"All right, we'll go together," Sabrina promised.

"I wish we were going there right now," Salem said. "You should bring Valerie along."

"I wish I could," Sabrina said wistfully.

"Your wish is my command," a voice replied. Sabrina looked down at the clay figurine her aunt Vesta had given her. It was talking! "Fasten your seat belts. It's gonna be a bumpy ride."

A carousel of colors and dancing shapes surrounded Sabrina, Salem, and Valerie as they whirled in a circle, faster and faster until everything became a blur. Then, just as if someone had thrown a hand brake, the entire whirling light show vanished and they tumbled out of the sky and into warm, soft sand.

Sabrina brushed the sand from her cheeks and rose up on her knees. Facing the opposite direction from the others, she caught her breath at the sight of three large pyramids reaching up into the twilight sky.

"Um, welcome to Egypt, I think," she said, biting her lower lip.

Sabrina, the Teenage Witch™ books

Available from ARCHWAY Paperbacks

Scarabian Nights

Nancy Holder

Based on Characters Appearing in Archie Comics

And based upon the television series
Sabrina, The Teenage Witch
Created for television by Nell Scovell
Developed for television by Jonathan Schmock

AN ARCHWAY PAPERBACK
Published by POCKET BOOKS
New York London Toronto Sydney Tokyo Singapore

AN ARCHWAY PAPERBACK *Original*

An Archway Paperback published by
POCKET BOOKS, a division of Simon & Schuster Inc.
1230 Avenue of the Americas, New York, NY 10020

ISBN: 0-671-02804-9

First Archway Paperback printing July 1999

10 9 8 7 6 5 4 3 2 1

Printed in the U.S.A.

IL: 4+

For Rebecca Morhaim,
a bit of magic in this realm

Scarabian Nights

☆

Chapter 1

☆

Tick. Tock. Tick. Tock.

Seated in the kitchen as the clock patiently counted out the long hours of the afternoon, Sabrina sighed and turned another page of *Young Witch* magazine. She skimmed the spell for a perpetually perfect manicure and yawned.

It was the first day of the second week of summer break, and she was already bored. It seemed that half of Westbridge High had already taken off for exotic adventures. Libby was in the south of France with her parents. Harvey and his teammates were attending football camp at Mark Clark College in Rhode Island.

From her jeans pocket, Sabrina pulled the

picture that her best friend, Valerie, had taken just before Harvey left for camp. In the photo he was in his uniform and Sabrina was smiling for the camera even though she'd been wistful that day, imagining a summer without him.

At least Sabrina still had Valerie to pal around with. But Valerie was no happier about the prospect of a dull summer than Sabrina was.

After tucking the photo back into her jeans pocket, Sabrina tugged on the spaghetti-strap T-shirt Valerie had given her when they were secret pals in cooking class last semester. Trouble was, Valerie had been so unsure about what to give her secret pal that she'd blurted out that she *was* Sabrina's secret pal and asked her what she would like as a secret pal gift. Which kind of violated the spirit of the exercise. But it had been awfully sweet of Valerie to care so much.

Tick. Tock.

Ding.

"Huh? Mmmf? Who's there? Guards!" cried a familiar voice from the backyard of the Spellmans' Victorian. "I'm being assassinated!"

"Salem, it's all right. Your timer went off," Sabrina called to him. "You were just dreaming."

Salem Saberhagen, the black cat who lived with her and her witchy aunts, Hilda and Zelda, was actually a warlock who had been transformed into a cat by the Witches' Council because he had tried to take over the mortal realm. He still dreamed of his glory days from time to time. And this was apparently one of those times.

Valerie, not knowing that the Spellmans were witches and having no idea that Salem was a former warlock, had purchased the spaghetti-strap T-shirt as Sabrina's secret pal gift because it was airbrushed with a drawing of a black cat that reminded Valerie of Salem. Sabrina considered that awfully thoughtful. But that was just how Valerie was.

Now Salem said, "Oh, a dream. Right." There was a pause. "My timer went off? That means this side is done. Would you mind helping me turn over? Oh, and could you reset the timer on your way out here?"

Sabrina chuckled. She flipped her magazine shut and got up from her chair. She smoothed her black track shorts as she passed the little round timer on the counter. She pointed and said,

Salem's catching lots of rays.
Add fifteen minutes to this tanning phase.

As the little white timer reset itself with a twist of its center dial, it drawled, "Just remember, Sabrina. Mr. Sun is not your friend."

"Got it," Sabrina said, smiling.

The kitchen timer had recently read an article about the hazards of tanning in *Good Witchkeeping,* and it was quite concerned about what all those bright ultraviolet rays might do to Salem's delicate feline skin.

Sabrina ambled into the backyard.

Salem no longer had any powers, but he could talk. Which he did, a lot, especially on the phone—and especially, it seemed, to Sabrina, whenever she was waiting for a call from Valerie or Harvey Kinkel, Sabrina's mortal boyfriend.

At the moment, however, Salem was not on the phone. He had on a pair of cat's-eye sunglasses and he appeared to be dozing. Between his forepaws, he held a large glass of iced tea. Beside his right paw was a copy of *Catmopolitan.* The edges of the magazine were curled.

"Just roll me over, if you please," he drawled. "I'm too worn out to do it myself."

"Worn out?" Sabrina asked in astonishment. "How can you be worn out? You haven't done anything all day." She added sadly, "And neither have I."

"Aw, cheer up," Salem said. "Have some of my favorite summer beverage. Icy and refreshing catnip tea."

"*Catnip* tea? No wonder you're so lazy," Sabrina said, as she pushed him over. "Catnip makes you drowsy, Salem. But that doesn't explain why you're so heavy."

"Catnip tea goes great with lemon meringue pie, that's why," he retorted, flicking his tail. "Actually, it goes great with anything."

"I see," she said, as she spied an empty pie tin beneath the hammock. She picked it up.

"And besides," Salem added, "I'm not heavy. I'm fluffy. Did you set the timer?"

"'Mr. Sun is not your friend,'" she said by way of answer.

Salem shook his head. "That timer is such a little worrywart. Last week it went on with some nonsense about snack foods and cholesterol levels."

She gave him a little pat. "It cares about you. All our appliances do."

"There are hardly any calories in lemon meringue pie," he sniffed. "It's almost all lemons."

"Uh-huh. Right." Sabrina looked down at the empty pan. "Did you really eat that whole pie?" Then she saw an empty wrapper for Little Wendy Witch's snack cakes on the other side of the hammock. "And an entire package of raspberry creme yodel-lady-hoo-hoo-hoos?"

"But enough about me," Salem said quickly. "Why the long face, Sabrina? No school, no worries."

"And nothing to do," she said. "I'm bored."

Salem blinked at her. *Bored?* You're a witch! With a flick of your finger, you could be in tanning in Tahiti. Or ice fishing in, well, Iceland.

Or snorkling in Hawaii. Hanauma Bay. Oh, the islands." He sighed. "You can scuba with fish swimming around you. *Hundreds* of them." His eyes glazed over. "Hundreds," he whispered to himself, as if he couldn't quite imagine such a thing. "And you could take me with you."

"Oh, Sabrina, there you are!" called a voice from the back door. It was Sabrina's aunt Zelda, elegantly dressed in a slit lavender skirt and a gray and lavender blouse. She was wearing her glasses and carrying a large stack of books. "I just got back from giving my first summer session lecture at the college."

"That's nice," Sabrina said.

Zelda's eyes shone. "I think I really got through to some of the students. Quantum physics just reaches down into your soul and transforms you. You know what I mean?"

"Um, okay," Sabrina said.

The last time something had transformed Sabrina—okay, the only time so far—was on the morning of her sixteenth birthday when she had discovered she was a witch. A half witch, actually, with a mortal mother and a warlock father. She had thought she'd been sent to live with her aunts because her mom had gone on an archaeological dig in Peru and that her father was in the foreign service. But actually, her aunts had taken charge of teaching Sabrina how to use her powers and to live responsibly in the mortal realm.

Whew. Not as easy as it sounds.

If quantum physics was anything like that, she might wait another year or two before she gave it a whirl. Still, maybe it would be fun. Her aunt sure liked it.

Zelda's smile was radiant. "I'm feeling so . . . *purposeful* today. Would you like some iced tea?"

Sabrina glanced at Salem, who appeared to have fallen asleep. "Catnip tea?" She didn't want anything that would make her feel any less energetic than she already was.

Zelda looked puzzled. "Of course not, dear. Orange pekoe."

"That'd be great." Sabrina turned to ask Salem if he'd like some, but he was snoring. It was so strange that someone would enjoy being bored. Salem positively relished it.

Sabrina trailed her aunt into the kitchen. The elegant witch had already propped one of her thick textbooks open and was reading it as she pointed at a spoon, which stirred sugar into a tall glass of tea. She was humming to herself. When she saw Sabrina, she looked up and said, "What's wrong, Sabrina? You look a little gloomy."

Sabrina shrugged. "I'd like to go somewhere, do something."

Aunt Zelda smiled. "But you can!"

"Yes, I know. Ice fishing. Hanauma Bay." She frowned a little. "I just want to go somewhere like a normal kid with my normal family."

With a gentle smiile, Zelda reached over and smoothed wisps of hair from Sabrina's forehead. "I understand. And we will."

"Woo-hoo! We will?" Sabrina asked hopefully.

"Yes." Zelda nodded. "Just as soon as I finish my lecture series and Hilda completes her Witches' Council duty. All right, dear?"

"Okay," Sabrina said, deflated. That would be weeks from now. Summer would be almost over.

"Good, dear," Zelda said. She had already gone back to reading her book.

The timer dinged. Sabrina said, "I need to tell Salem his side's done."

"Oh, and don't forget to feed him, dear," Zelda called after her.

Sabrina sighed. Feeding Salem had become one of her official chores. Today it would probably be the only productive thing she did.

"Hey, Salem," she said, heading for the hammock.

Then *poof!* The entire backyard was magically transformed into a colorful Middle Eastern bazaar. Exotic woven rugs flapped in the breeze on ropes strung between two tall palm trees. Men in long white robes and women draped with veils thronged several stalls, examining woven bowls brimming with pomegranates, figs, and dates. The spicy scent of sandalwood filled the air.

As Sabrina stared, the throng parted to reveal a belly-dancing troupe—three women in spangled tops and silky skirts. Tiny cymbals clashed and jingled on their fingertips. A man in a turban played a drum while another blew on a flute.

"Aunt Zelda?" Sabrina called. "Did you do this to cheer me up?"

Accompanied by the clang of a gong, a bald giant dressed in a leopard-skin leotard and leather sandals appeared in the midst of all the clamor. He clapped his hands and cried, "Life, health, prosperity to Vesta! May she live a thousand thousand years!"

An elephant popped into view behind the giant. Seated on its back in an elaborate velvet chair was Sabrina's third aunt, the pleasure-loving Vesta. The glamorous auburn-haired witch was swathed in an elegant khaki shirt and flared skirt, complemented by dainty-heeled leather boots. From her pith helmet streamed a long white gauzy scarf, which was carried behind the elephant by a small boy in a gray robe and a cone-shaped red hat with a flat top.

"It's Vesta! Behold the beautiful Vesta!" the belly dancers sang, bowing deeply.

Vesta waved and blew Sabrina a kiss. As Sabrina clapped her hands in delight, the elephant knelt, and Vesta gracefully dismounted by placing her boot in the elephant's trunk and urging it to set her gently on the ground.

"Aunt Vesta!" Sabrina said happily.

Sabrina hurried toward her. Vesta threw her arms around her niece and kissed her forehead.

"Sabrina, my darling!" she cried. "I've just returned from the pyramids. I'm on my way back to the Other Realm and I just dropped in to give you the most adorable little souvenir."

With a flourish she took the lid off a little straw basket and pulled out a small clay statuette the size of Sabrina's hand. It was a figure of a man wearing a short skirt. He held his right hand over his heart, as if he were reciting the Pledge of Allegiance. His features were painted on, his eyes were outlined in black, and he sported a rather modern-looking goatee, which didn't do much for him, in Sabrina's opinion.

"It's called a *ushabti,*" Vesta explained. "The ancient Egyptians were just crazy about them. They made thousands of them."

"It's very nice," Sabrina said a little uncertainly. "I'll put it on my knickknack shelf."

"No, no, no." Vesta wagged her finger. "This is a magical present. You see, each *ushabti* was created to perform a specific task for its owner. One might bake bread, another would herd the geese, and yet another could catch fish."

"Did someone say fish?" Salem asked excitedly, his head poking out of another basket. "Does ours catch fish? Say, tuna?"

Vesta laughed. "No, Salem. Not exactly. But it just so happens that this *ushabti* belonged to the cat goddess, Bast. She created it to feed one of her household cats. Of which she had hundreds, I might add."

"My kind of woman," Salem said eagerly.

"Woo-hoo!" Sabrina cried. "A way to get out of doing my chore!"

"Exactly." Vesta beamed at her. "You're as smart as you are pretty, Sabrina."

Salem shook his head in awe. "I swear you're psychic, Vesta. This little guy is exactly what Sabrina needs."

"I'm just a doting auntie." Vesta chucked Sabrina under the chin. "Next time I go to Egypt, do you want to come with me? Even better, we could travel back to the time of the pharaohs—ancient Egypt." She smiled brightly. "You'd love it. The clothes were to die for, and people wore beautiful cornrow wigs with gold flowers in them."

Sabrina clutched the *ushabti*. "Yes, Aunt Vesta. I'd love to go with you. I'll go grab my purse and—"

"Then we will go," Vesta announced. "Soon. But for now"—she yawned—"I'm due for a facial, a manicure, a pedicure, an herbal wrap, and a nice long nap. Egypt is fascinating, but it's also very sandy, and the hot sun tires you out."

"Can I relate," Salem said, also yawning.

"All right, Aunt Vesta." Sabrina rose up on tiptoe and kissed her aunt on the cheek. "Thanks again."

"My pleasure." Vesta airily waved her hands. "But then, all of life is a pleasure."

She snapped her fingers, and she, the belly dancers, the rugs, the elephant, and everything else trooped through the back door and into the Spellman mansion. Sabrina waited for Zelda's protests that the parade was tracking in dirt, but there was nothing. She sighed. Her other aunt was probably still engrossed in her physics book, and likely to remain that way for the rest of the day.

A few seconds later, Sabrina heard the thunderclap that signaled the use of their linen closet, which doubled as a passageway to and from the Other Realm.

Aunt Vesta had returned to her pleasure dome.

Well, Zelda might be busy, but at least Sabrina was left with an interesting new magical way to feed Salem.

"So this day wasn't a total wash," she said to the figure.

"Let's put him through his paces," Salem urged. "I'm starving."

"You're always starving," Sabrina said.

"True." Salem batted a paw toward the statue. "But as this *ushabti* is my witness, I'll never be hungry again."

"Hmm. I can see I'm going to have to have a talk with him," Sabrina said. "Maybe he and I can teach you to eat more nutritiously."

She looked directly into the painted eyes of the figurine. The eyes seemed to glitter merrily back at her.

"So maybe all kinds of neat things will happen this summer," she said.

Woo-hoo! Why not?

☆

Chapter 2

☆

As Sabrina prepared to go inside and show the *ushabti* where Salem's cat food was kept, Aunt Zelda waved to her from the back door. With her glasses perched on her nose, Zelda was still reading her physics book, carrying it in her right hand.

"Sabrina," she said without looking up from the page. "Valerie's here to see you."

"Coming, Aunt Zelda," Sabrina said.

Salem and Sabrina went into the kitchen. There stood Valerie, who smiled at Zelda as she left the room, her nose still in her book

"Sabrina!" she said excitedly. "Guess what! There's a sneak preview of *I Know You Know I Saw You Screaming Last Semester*. It starts in twenty minutes. If we hurry, we can get in."

"Oh, cool!" Sabrina cried.

"Oh, puh-leez," Salem murmured quietly, so that only Sabrina could hear. Then he raised his eyebrows and whispered, "Can I come, too? Can I, huh? Can I?"

The timer dinged.

"Do you have something in the oven?" Valerie asked, turning to look.

"Um, cookies," Sabrina said, pointing surreptitiously. "Could you check them?"

"Wow. Don't you think it's a little too hot for baking?" Valerie asked, opening the oven door. The delicious scent of freshly baked cookies filled the air.

"Pretty please?" Salem persisted.

"No," Sabrina whispered back. "They won't let you into the theater. But I'll tell you all about it when I get home."

"Yum, chocolate chip. They're done." Still with her back to Salem and Sabrina, Valerie reached for an oven mitt.

"Shucks. I never get to go anywhere," Salem pouted. Then he brightened. "Ancient Egypt would be good, though. When you go there, I want to go, too."

"All right, we'll go together," Sabrina promised.

"I wish we were going there right now," Salem said. "You should bring Valerie along."

"I wish I could," Sabrina said wistfully.

"Your wish is my command," a voice replied. Sabrina looked down at the clay figurine. It was talking! "Fasten your seat belts. It's gonna be a bumpy ride."

"Hey, wait a minute!" Sabrina protested.

But it was too late. A carousel of colors and dancing shapes surrounded Sabrina, Salem, and Valerie as they whirled in a circle, faster and faster until everything became a blur.

Valerie started screaming and Salem said calmly, "This takes me back to the Tivoli Gardens, the amusement park in Denmark. I was about to conquer Copenhagen, but first all my generals and I went on the roller coaster. I got sick. Had to cancel the entire battle campaign."

"Sabrina, what's going on? What's happening?" Valerie shrieked.

"Prepare for landing," the *ushabti* announced.

"What?" Sabrina demanded.

Then, just as if someone had thrown a hand brake, the entire whirling light show vanished and Sabrina, Valerie, Salem, and the statuette tumbled out of the sky and into warm, soft sand.

"Wow, what a trip!" Salem said, shaking himself off as he wobbled to his feet. "That should be a ride at Disneyland."

"Thank you," the *ushabti* answered. It, too, stood up and dusted itself off. It bowed in Salem's direction. "These days I get more complaints than compliments when I grant the wishes of my masters."

"People have lost their sense of adventure," Salem sniffed, licking his fur.

"Is that thing talking?" Valerie shouted as she staggered to her feet. She was shaking. Tears of panic streamed down her cheeks. "Is Salem talking? Sabrina, where are we?"

Sabrina brushed the sand from her cheeks and rose up on her knees. Facing the opposite direction from the others, she caught her breath at the sight of three large pyramids reaching up into the twilight sky.

"Um, welcome to Egypt, I think," she said, biting her lower lip.

"Give that little girl a hand-wrung pheasant," the *ushabti* said cheerily. "This is ancient Egypt, as a matter of fact." He spread his arms. "My hometown and my home time."

Sabrina turned to her friend. "Valerie, I'm sorry, but I think we're going to miss the movie."

In reply, Valerie keeled over in a dead faint.

"Wanna see what I do for an encore?" the *ushabti* asked jauntily.

"Yes, indeed I do, especially if it involves food," Salem said happily.

The *ushabti* bowed and replied, "Let's call this the appetizer."

And soon they were spinning off again amid whirling colors and lights.

The next thing Sabrina knew, she and the others were unceremoniously dropped onto the hard stone floor of an enormous room. Columns rose maybe twenty feet to support an elaborately painted ceiling depicting hundreds of cats at some kind of a festival, all of them in silhouette, some larger than the others and standing on two legs while dozens of others served them from platters piled high with food and urns filled with drink. Still others were dancing and playing small drums and flutes.

The walls also showed cats, all in profile, doing all kinds of things: leaping at balls of white yarnlike stuff, perched on a riverbank batting at bright orange fish in the water, being brushed by other cats. And around the perimeter of the room stood dozens of stone statues of cats, all very majestic and lifelike.

Most remarkable of all, however, was that the large room was overflowing with cats. Real cats. Tortoiseshell cats. Short-haired Abyssinians. Black cats with blue eyes. Blue cats with black eyes. White cats.

"Oh, my, oh, my," Salem gasped. "We have definitely died and gone to heaven."

Sabrina frowned at him. "Salem, don't you dare faint on me. I've already got Valerie to deal with."

They both looked down at Valerie, who was lying on the floor with her eyes closed. Valerie moaned and said, "Mom, did my alarm go off?"

"Maybe she thinks she's dreaming," Sabrina said hopefully.

"I think I am, too," Salem said, blinking at the sights around him.

Sabrina went on, "Maybe we can keep her thinking that until we figure out a way to get back to Westbridge."

"Who wants to leave?" Salem snorted, taking in the view of all the cats.

"Then I've pleased you, master?" the *ushabti* asked Salem with a little bow.

"Master." Salem closed his eyes. "How I've longed to hear someone call me that again."

"Master. Master, master, master," said the *ushabti*.

Salem groaned with delight.

"Wait a minute." Sabrina bent down and picked the figurine up. "All you're supposed to be is a cat feeder."

"No," the *ushabti* said, chuckling as he stroked his goatee. "I'm a cat *pleaser*. Your aunt

19

got her Arabic nouns all mixed up. It's charming, her rotten Arabic."

"Give reverence to her Divine Whiskerness!" someone shouted.

Sabrina and Salem turned toward the voice while the *ushabti* murmured, "Gulp," and ran behind Sabrina's leg.

A bald man wearing an off-the-shoulder leopard-skin ensemble smacked a staff on the stone floor. His eyes were almond-shaped and yellow, like Salem's, and his ears were triangles, like Salem's. His face was long, his cheekbones high, and he had whiskers that extended from either side of his small, triangular nose.

He looked like a cat!

Behind him, at the far end of the room, on a platform, a tall woman slunk toward a jeweled throne that was shaped like the open mouth of a giant lion. The gleaming white teeth framed her most impressively as she climbed onto the large seat and curled up on it with her legs to one side. She glowed with a strange golden light, and when she moved, she seemed to blur just the slightest bit. Her eyes were also almond-shaped and yellow. Her other features were very catlike, including little cat ears on either side of a heavy black wig of cornrows. Her clothes were made of velvet printed to resemble the markings of a calico cat, and over her fingernails she wore claws made of gold. Or maybe they were her real claws.

"You strangers!" the man bellowed. "Identify yourselves."

"We're, um . . ." Sabrina began. She whispered to the *ushabti*, "I could use some help here."

"Try, 'I am Dorothy, meek and mild,'" Salem suggested.

"I'm Sabrina Spellman," Sabrina said.

"Ah, the handmaiden," the woman said. She raised her hand and pointed with her gold nails at the airbrushed cat on Sabrina's T-shirt. "I see by the markings on your shirt that you belong to this exquisite specimen of a cat."

Sabrina blinked. "Excuse me?"

As the cat-woman gazed at Salem, she purred. "And you, exquisite specimen, what is your name?"

"Salem," he replied.

"Ah." She moved her shoulders. "Come forward, you big, beautiful cat," she commanded regally, raking the air.

She smiled at Sabrina. "You may approach as well, pale maiden."

"Thank you," Sabrina said. The oven timer would be pleased to hear her called a pale maiden. That meant she hadn't spent too much time lying in the sun.

She cast an anxious glance at Valerie. "What about my friend?"

"She shall be tended to," the woman said, clapping her hands.

Immediately, four sturdy men carrying a couch upholstered in what appeared to be leopard skin marched into the room. They were bald and wore leather sandals and short flared skirts made of stiff white fabric. They also had almond-shaped eyes, triangular ears, small pink noses, and long whiskers.

The catlike men set the couch down and gently lifted Valerie onto it. Then they marched away, leaving Valerie behind, resting on the couch.

Valerie murmured, "Just five more minutes, Mom, okay?"

"Delightful Royalness," the *ushabti* said, bowing low, "I have brought these travelers across the sands of time."

The woman looked down at him, wrinkling her nose in distaste. "An amazing feat, Myron."

Myron?

"Amazing in that at last you have done something right," the cat-woman said disdainfully. "It shall be recorded in the annals of history, since it's the *only* thing you've ever done right."

"Thank you, O Great One." Myron sighed unhappily and bowed again.

The woman returned her attention to Salem and Sabrina. "You must be hungry and thirsty."

"Yes, yes, we're starving," Salem assured her. "We're just fainting with hunger."

"Salem," Sabrina chided.

The golden-eyed woman beamed at Salem. "Then you shall dine as you have never dined before."

Again she clapped her hands. In an instant, a procession of women in black cornrow wigs similar to hers and wearing gauzy white robes appeared. They, too, resembled cats, and their turquoise and lapis necklaces reminded Sabrina of collars. One carried a bowl of fresh milk; another, a dish of dried squid; a third, a platter of sardines.

"Well, she was right," Sabrina murmured, feeling queasy. "I've never dined like this before."

"Be polite," Salem said eagerly.

"Pillows for our guests," the cat-woman commanded.

Two more cat-people approached, bowed low before Salem and Sabrina, and fluffed up large satin pillows for them to sit on.

"Curl up," the woman invited them. "Make yourselves comfortable."

Salem made an elaborate show of kneading himself a nice area in the large pillow. Then he stretched forward and backward, and plopped down just as one of the cat-girls held out a copper bowl of cream. Sabrina sat cross-legged.

The glowing cat-woman dipped her face toward the bowl and daintily lapped up some milk.

"Does the food delight you?" she asked, coming up for air.

"And how," Salem said. "Thank you."

"Yes, thank you," Sabrina added.

"Then I am filled with pleasure," the woman said, and purred.

Salem sighed. "Sabrina, is it just me, or is she the most beautiful thing you've ever laid eyes on?" He lapped up some milk. "And isn't this just the best food? It even beats the all-you-can-eat buffet at the Westbridge Yummyteria!"

"You don't get out enough," Sabrina muttered.

"I've been trying to tell you that." He glanced around. "But I'm sure this beats *I Know You Know I Saw You Screaming in Gym Class*."

"*Last Semester,*" Sabrina corrected him.

"You have gym every semester."

Just then one of the cat-girls held out to Sabrina a small earthenware dish with a whole dead fish on it.

"Please, enjoy, *meow,*" she said.

"Thanks so much, but I'm not very hungry,"

Sabrina said apologetically as she put her hands in her lap.

Salem twitched his tail. "Now, now, be polite. Just try a taste. Isn't that what your mother used to tell you when you were a little girl?"

"That was for people food," Sabrina protested.

"Hey, when in Rome, eat like an Egyptian."

The *ushabti* tiptoed up to the right rear corner of Sabrina's pillow and climbed aboard. "I think you two have made a nice first impression," he said, nodding. "That's good."

"Who is she?" Sabrina whispered to him.

Salem said, "Yes, tell us her name. And her address. And her phone number."

"We don't have phones," the *ushabti* informed him. "They haven't been invented yet."

"Then she probably doesn't have a Web site, either," Salem pouted. "Too bad. I'd love to download some pictures of her to have for my very own."

The *ushabti* shook his head. "No Web site." He cleared his throat, sounding a little nervous. "But she is beautiful, isn't she?" the little figurine said, sighing. "She's one in a million, that gorgeous thing. She's my queen." He sighed. "Otherwise known as Bast, the cat goddess."

"Get out," Sabrina said excitedly. "She's a real live goddess?"

"It all makes sense now." Salem looked adoringly at the goddess as she daintily selected a squid, held it high above her mouth, tipped back her head, and dropped it in. After chewing a few times, she licked her lips, then her nose, and smiled contentedly.

She stood and spread her hands. At once everybody in the room dropped to the floor.

"Know me," she said to Sabrina and Salem. "I am the ruler of this place. I am—"

"The cat goddess Bast," Salem interrupted dreamily.

She lowered her hands and looked at him intently. "You know of me?"

"Of course." He shrugged. "Who doesn't? You're the most beautiful goddess in all of ancient Egypt."

"Oh, brother," Sabrina muttered.

"Oh." She smiled brilliantly. "Court magician!" she cried, clapping her hands. "Appear!"

"A magician!" Sabrina said brightly. "Cool." She'd have liked to chat with him, compare notes on magic, maybe collect a couple of neat spells.

Suddenly a catlike man with extremely long white hair and a flowing white beard zapped into the room in a dramatic puff of purple smoke. Spangles rippled through the air as he bowed low before the woman, raking the air with his hands. He wore a shiny black robe with enormous sleeves. It was decorated with silver moons and stars. A gigantic silver turban decorated with feathers and jewels covered his head. It looked like an expanded Jiffy Pop popcorn ball.

From the back of his robe, a tail flicked in the air.

He said in a high, nasal voice, "O most regal whiskered goddess, what is your wish and what is your delight?"

The woman pointed at Salem. "Take his measure. He is the one."

The man blinked his catlike blue eyes at Salem, looking him over. "At once, O most meowfulness. And a very wise choice, may I say, O great goddess most wise."

Salem's eyelids fluttered. "Sabrina!" he gushed. "I'm the one!"

"Uh-oh," Myron the *ushabti* murmured.

"Uh-oh?" Sabrina echoed, frowning at Myron. "Uh-oh, why?"

"Oh, nothing, nothing," he said innocently.

"Uh-uh *what?*" Sabrina persisted.

"Nothing," Myron insisted, keeping his eyes wide and innocent.

"Uh-uh *who?*"

The *ushabti* laughed shakily. "Really, Sabrina, it's nothing at all, especially for someone like you." He made his fingers go in little circles. "A magic someone."

Sabrina was doubtful. She replied, "Okay, if you say so." But it didn't sound like nothing.

Then she realized there was one more question she hadn't asked. So she asked it.

"Uh-oh *when?*"

"Tonight," Myron blurted. Then he covered his mouth and said, "Whoops."

Uh-oh.

☆

Chapter 3

☆

As Sabrina watched from her pillow in Bast's throne room, the court magician swirled over toward Salem. His hair streamed around him like a miniature tornado. Wherever he went, he trailed spangles and little glowing bits of magic.

Growing closer, he began to slink toward the big black cat, as if Salem were a mouse or a nice open can of tuna and he were a stealthy or very hungry Persian cat. Sabrina did not like the look of that slink. But Salem didn't notice. He was mesmerized by Bast, and he was smiling up at her as if *she* were a nice open can of tuna.

At the goddess's pleased expression and a wave of her hand, the magician snapped his fingers so loud that Sabrina jumped. In a flash of golden light, something very like a yardstick appeared in his hands—except that instead of inches and feet, it was covered with strange little symbols that looked like cat whiskers and cat paws.

"Stand up straight, please," he said to Salem. "Accuracy is vital."

Eagerly Salem rose up and lifted his chin. "Then let me assure you that I just look short," he told the magician as he posed like a hunting dog, er, cat. "I'm actually very tall."

"Oh, I can see that," the man replied. He clapped his hands and the measuring stick vanished. "Twenty paws and two whiskers. Very good. Thank you."

He approached Bast and bowed deeply. "I have what I need to begin, O most short-haired."

"You also have very little time," she told him. "Tonight is *the night.*"

He nodded. "Be assured that I'll toil without ceasing to obey your command," he said, bowing so low that his turban appeared to be in danger of falling off. Sabrina was about to point it into place when he straightened up and looked directly at her.

"I almost forgot about you," he said. He snapped his fingers again, and again the measuring stick materialized. As she swallowed, he began to measure her as well.

"Hey, what are you doing?" she asked nervously. *"I'm* not the one." She wrinkled her nose. "Am I?"

"Hush," the magician said. "I need to concentrate."

"Why?" Sabrina asked.

He ignored her. Suddenly she felt kind of strange all over, as if someone had turned the air conditioning up a little too high. She shivered once, twice, three times.

"Cold?" the magician queried politely.

"Yes, I am," Sabrina replied.

"Good," he said.

Then, with another dramatic snap of his fingers and a puff of purple smoke, he vanished.

Bast turned her attention back to Salem. "If you have quieted the rumbling of your stomach, then come to me, you exquisite creature, and sit beside me on my throne."

"Me-*ow,"* Salem said.

With that, he flicked his tail at Sabrina and trotted toward the throne.

"Hoo, boy," Myron muttered to Sabrina. "Here we go again."

"What do you mean?" Sabrina asked. She pointed at him. "And don't you try that 'Oh, nothing' routine on me again. My finger's armed and pointed at you. If you don't tell me what's going on, I'm going to do something you won't like!" She had no idea what that would be, and she wasn't very good at making threats, anyway.

"Oh, no, not camel cleanup detail again!" he groaned. "All right, I'll talk." He made a face. "Let's just say my exquisite mistress goes through suitors faster than your cat there goes through squid-and-fish-head pizzas."

"Huh? How do you know so much about us?" she asked.

He shrugged. "I did an instant dossier when your aunt Vesta presented me to you. I'm magical, remember?"

Sabrina shrugged. "Well, when she decides she doesn't want Salem to be her suitor anymore, we'll just go home."

"Wrong," the *ushabti* said. He gestured to the dozens of cat statues. "See those?"

Sabrina gulped. "Yes?"

"Those were once living cat-guys. They were boyfriends who became fiancés who became husbands who became stone statues." He dropped his voice. "The poor woman just doesn't know what she's looking for. She's confused. Conflicted."

"Salem," Sabrina called out anxiously. "Ah, we need to get going. Your Goddessness, we hate to eat and run, but—"

Salem had just reached the base of the throne. The glowing woman reached down and held something small and brown. It looked like a plus sign with an oval on top.

"Behold!" she said.

All the cat-people and all the cats said, *"Mrrrow."* Those with hands applauded.

"Don't eat it," Myron whispered to Salem, but the warlock-turned-cat was too far away to hear him.

"Why not?" Sabrina asked anxiously.

The goddess picked Salem up and put the object in his mouth.

"Oh, boy. Whatever that is, it's *good,"* Salem gushed, chewing appreciatively.

"Uh-oh," the *ushabti* moaned again. "That was *ankh* bread. It's the first step."

"First step?" Sabrina asked, alarmed.

He held up three clay fingers. "Three bites and he'll be pledged to her. The first bite's like a promise ring. Second one's like an engagement ring. Third"—he frowned unhappily— "marriage."

"Do you have any more?" Salem asked the goddess, licking his face.

"It's a rare Egyptian sweet," Bast said. "I shall give you another bite in three hours. And tonight, the Night of the Scarab Moon, a third tender morsel shall pass your whiskers."

"Oh, no," Sabrina said. Then she looked down at Myron. "That's the 'when' that you mentioned, isn't it? When he eats the third bite, he'll be married to her!"

"Well, yes, that's about right," Myron murmured.

At that very moment, Valerie sat up, looked around, and opened her mouth to scream.

"Easy, easy," Sabrina said to Valerie. "It's okay."

Valerie was wild-eyed as she took in her surroundings. "It's *okay*? This is *okay*? Whose dictionary are we using to look up that word?"

"Well," Sabrina said, "a lot has happened since you, um, hit your head and went into a coma for years and years. Here in the future we dress like ancient Egyptians. We've also given cats implants so they can talk. Like Salem there. Plus some people think they are goddesses."

"Oh, man, is that lame," Myron said, shaking his head.

Valerie's eyes got even wider as she stared at the talking clay statuette.

"And we also have animated dolls," Sabrina pressed on. "So very lifelike, isn't it?"

Valerie blinked. She looked around. She said, "I'm sorry, Sabrina, but I really do have to do a little screaming here."

"Okay, listen," the *ushabti* said. "I'm a magical ancient Egyptian figurine. Sabrina's aunt came to Egypt and brought me back as a present. You were transported back here because your cat expressed a desire to visit ancient Egypt. And Bast, the goddess of cats, has fallen in love with him." He looked at Sabrina as if to say, *See how the experts do it?*

"Oh." Valerie looked around, smiling happily. "A magical figurine, eh? And a cat goddess. That's cool." She raised an eyebrow at Sabrina. "Why didn't you just tell me the truth? Who'd believe all that stuff about a coma?"

"Anyone who watches soap operas," Sabrina said glumly. To Myron she muttered, "You should run for political office."

"I have," he said proudly. "And I won. I was the mayor of Cairo for two hundred years." He grew wistful. "And then the reigning pharaoh instituted term limits and I was out of a job."

"Hark, your other handmaiden has awakened," Bast said to Salem. She gestured to Valerie.

"Huh? Oh, yeah. Hi, Valerie. Have a snack."

Valerie swayed. "Salem really *is* talking."

"Uh, that would be a yes," Sabrina replied anxiously.

"Faint, scream," Valerie said. "I've always been a little on the indecisive side."

Salem went on, "The fish heads are great, and the ankh bread is to die for."

Myron murmured, "Yeah, no kidding."

As Bast set Salem beside her on the fat throne pillow, he moaned with bliss. Languidly she scratched him behind the ears, and he flopped onto his side.

"Give the revived handmaiden food and drink," she commanded her servants.

A cat-girl approached Valerie with a bowl of milk and a saucer of fish heads.

Valerie's face puckered up. Sabrina was certain she was going to let out an earsplitting shriek, so she surreptitiously pointed and gave Valerie a quick pinch of silent treatment.

Valerie looked startled when no sound came out of her mouth. She touched her throat and tried again.

Sabrina hurried over to her and said, "Valerie, stay calm. We'll figure out a way to get out of here."

"That's good," Valerie said numbly. "That's really good."

Bast resumed scratching Salem behind the ears. "Ah, you handsome tiger, you," she said warmly. "Let's stroll around my lotus pond together, shall we?"

Salem eagerly kneaded the seat of the throne with his claws. "But of course. Wild Siamese and centurions' sandals couldn't keep me from your side, beautiful lady," Salem replied.

The goddess rose. Everyone fell back onto the floor.

"Boy, Sabrina, this is weird," Valerie said. "Are you sure I'm not dreaming?"

Sabrina took a breath and glanced at Myron, who said, "Don't even try it. You're a lousy liar."

"I am not," Sabrina shot back. "I'm a very

good liar. Just ask Salem." She raised her head. "Oh, Salem?"

All she saw was the very tip of the black cat's tail as he made a grand exit out the side door.

"This is your fault," Sabrina told the *ushabti*. "You brought us here."

"Yes, I did." Myron shrugged unhappily. "But look on the bright side. With any luck, she won't turn either of *you* into stone statues. Just your cat, eventually."

"Just my cat," Sabrina echoed hollowly. "Oh, gee, that's nice to know."

What on earth was she going to do?

As if to answer her, Valerie said, "First I'm going to throw up, then I'm going to scream, and then I think I'll faint again. In that order, I hope."

"What on earth am I going to do?" Zelda asked. She was looking at a list of possible titles for her quantum physics lecture. She couldn't decide between "The Uncertainty Principle, Maybe, for Sure" and "Quantum Electrodynamics: Friend, Foe, or Casual Acquaintance?"

"Sabrina dear, which one do you like best?" she asked aloud. When there was no answer, she called out again. "Sabrina?"

Still staring at her physics textbook, she turned off the computer and pushed away from her desk.

She sighed and checked her watch. It was almost six, and she was hungry. She had smelled cookies baking a while before. Maybe she'd just have one before dinner. Maybe two.

"Sabrina?" she called as she walked into the kitchen. "I'm going to raid the cookie jar. All right?" On occasion, Sabrina baked yummy goodies for various school functions, and Zelda wanted to make sure there wasn't a prior claim on these little gems. They smelled heavenly. "Dear?"

Maybe Sabrina wasn't in the house. A small, anxious voice tugged at the back of Zelda's mind. She did recall that Valerie had come by, but she, Zelda, had been so engrossed in preparing for her physics lecture that she hadn't paid close attention to her niece or her friend. Maybe they had gone treasure-hunting in the basement. But Sabrina as a rule didn't take mortals down there. There was too much evidence that the Spellmans were witches—boxes labeled "Grandma's Old Cauldrons," for example, and crates of memorabilia with labels like "Hilda's Stuff, 16TH Century. Keep Thy Mitts Off."

She crossed to the cookie jar, plucked out a cookie, and called, "Salem? Do you know where Sabrina and Valerie are?"

There was no answer.

She frowned slightly. "Salem?"

Nothing.

"Oh, Salem," she called, "there are freshly baked cookies." If he was in the house, that was certain to bring him running.

It didn't.

Zelda frowned and munched the cookie thoughtfully. Sabrina had complained about being bored and having nothing to look forward to this summer. Same with Valerie. And Salem, a housebound house cat, was always itching to travel—unless he was itching from fleas, which was highly unlikely, since Zelda bathed him so often that he had threatened to complain to the Humane Society.

Was it possible the three of them had gone off together to have an adventure?

If so, they should be home soon.

She smiled to herself and picked up her physics text.

But the next thing she knew, it was an hour later and a brief search of the house yielded no Sabrina, no Valerie, and no Salem.

Now she was a little worried. She wondered if they'd gone to Valerie's house after all. Should she call Valerie's mother?

This was one of those sticky spots witches with nieces of high school age sometimes found themselves in. If Valerie was with Sabrina and they were missing, there was a good chance that something magical had happened—not magical in the Matt Damon sense, but something that

Zelda would not be able to share with a mortal. Witches who lived in the mortal realm were under strict orders by the Witches' Council not to let anyone know that such a thing as witches existed, much less reveal that they were witches themselves.

She reminded herself that Sabrina was becoming quite a mature young witch.

Zelda went back to reading.

Two more hours passed, and still no Sabrina. Zelda made a few calls to friends, but no one had seen Sabrina or Valerie. She transported herself over to Valerie's house and peeked in the family room, the kitchen, and Valerie's room. No luck. She tried the Slicery and went all through the mall. Still no girls.

When she got back home, there was still no sign of Sabrina.

A little more concerned, she wrote a note to the head of the Witches' Council and popped it into the toaster, as that was the way the Spellmans communicated with the other realm. Her note said: "May it please the council, Zelda Spellman requests permission to discuss a personal situation with her sister, Hilda Spellman."

She popped it in the toaster, pushed down the lever, and drummed her fingers on the countertop as the note disappeared. For a few minutes, she stared at the appliance, awaiting a reply. Then, realizing that a watched toaster never pops, she plucked another cookie from the cookie jar and left the kitchen.

Sure enough, as soon as she reached the stairs, she heard the telltale sound of a return memo. She hurried back into the kitchen and pulled it from the toaster.

The memo read, "No way, José. She's too busy."

She slumped. "Well, at least they got right to the point," she said, disappointed.

Zelda sighed.

She was on her own.

☆

Chapter 4

☆

In Bast's throne room, Sabrina sighed and looked at Valerie. "I guess we're on our own," she said.

"Does that mean I get to scream now?" Valerie asked.

"Handmaidens!" a voice boomed.

They both jumped.

A man with very sharp, catlike facial features, wearing a huge beaded collar of turquoise, yellow, red, and dark blue, clapped his hands three times and pointed at Sabrina and Valerie. "I am the goddess's grand vizier. You will be escorted to your room. There you will await the pleasure of your master."

"Huh?" Valerie said. "Master?"

"He means Salem," Sabrina whispered. "Everybody thinks we're his servants because of my T-shirt."

Valerie groaned. "I *knew* I should have gotten you a gift certificate to the Slicery instead of that shirt. I couldn't decide."

Sabrina's stomach grumbled. What she wouldn't give for some good, hot food that wasn't topped with bait. "Oh, I really like the shirt," she assured her friend. "It really does look just like Salem."

"Which is the problem," Valerie groaned.

"There was no way to know that we'd end up in ancient Egypt in a roomful of cat people when you bought it," Sabrina reminded her.

Just then, Sabrina and Valerie were approached by tall, lion like cat guards carrying spears.

"Um, Myron?" Sabrina squeaked. But the *ushabti* was gone.

"Let's go," one of the guards said to Sabrina.

Sabrina thought about pointing and whisking Valerie and herself back home, but they couldn't leave without Salem. So she kept her hands folded as she allowed the cat-men to escort her and Valerie out of the room.

They were taken through a maze of corridors and passageways, all elaborately decorated with paintings of all kinds of cat. A border of cats's eyes heavily lined in black topped most of the walls. Others featured decorative panels of fish.

"I should have gone snorkeling," Sabrina muttered, "or toured a live volcano or something."

Valerie, who didn't hear her, swallowed hard and said, "Sabrina, we'll never find our way out of here."

"Oh, yes, we will," Sabrina said. This time, she did point, planning to leave a trail of invisible bread crumbs for them to follow later. Invisible to mortals, anyway.

But when she pointed, nothing happened.

Surprised, she blinked, checked her finger, and pointed again.

"Sabrina, is something wrong?" Valerie asked. "I mean, something else?"

"Um," Sabrina murmured.

Then one of the guards said, "You will wait for your master here." He was very tall, towering over the girls like a man on stilts.

He stopped in front of an enormous door decorated with a huge portrait of Bast made of stones. The doorknob was a replica of Bast's hand with its golden nails.

"Okay, yes, sir," Valerie said, while Sabrina tried another spell, this one to create a gentle breeze in the passageway.

Again nothing happened.

The tall guard opened the door. She and

44

Valerie walked into a room that gleamed with gold—gold statues, large gold lotuses that seemed to rise from the mosaic floor, and gold sconces from which torches flickered and smoked.

"This is definitely not Kansas," Valerie muttered as she looked around. "But it could pass for Caesar's Palace in a pinch."

"When were you in Caesar's Palace?" Sabrina asked.

Valerie shrugged. "When you don't date much—or rather, ever—you have a lot of time to watch infomercials. One of my favorites is about Las Vegas."

"Oh, I know what you mean. One of my favorites is about Mars. They have really great, um, red rocks there." She had managed to stop herself in time from blurting out that the infomercial was actually about the skiing on Mars, which really *was* great; she'd gone there with her aunts on a vacation. Back when they took vacations.

Not that she would ever complain about the lack of vacations again. Not in front of magical figurines, anyway.

"Our mistress has provided you with suitable raiment," another of the guards said.

Valerie frowned.

The man indicated two lovely gauze robes

strung on a sort of clothes line. On a stand beside each one, elaborate black wigs of cornrows and golden headbands gleamed in the torchlight from the walls.

Without further ado, the guards trooped out. Valerie looked at Sabrina, and Sabrina looked at Valerie. Sabrina said, "Let's put on the clothes. We'll fit in better."

"Yeah, except we don't look like cats," Valerie pointed out.

"Yeah." Sabrina glanced down at her finger. If her magic were working, it would be a simple matter to alter their appearance. But it wasn't working.

Why not?

The girls changed their clothes. As Sabrina folded her jeans, she remembered the photo of her and Harvey and pulled it out to look at it, wondering when, and if, she would ever see him again. Meanwhile, Valerie frowned at herself in a beautiful golden hand mirror and tugged at her wig, saying, "Are my cornrows straight? I'm not sure, but I think I have this thing on backwards."

"I must say, you're taking all this rather well," Sabrina told her as she helped Valerie with her hairpiece. "I'm on the verge of wigging out."

Valerie smiled. She touched her lapis and turquoise necklace and the matching bracelet.

"Well, there's jewelry involved," she said. "That's a plus, don't you think?"

Seeing Sabrina's surprise, Valerie shook her head. "Oh, Sabrina, please. Do you have any idea how freaked out I am? I'll throw your own words back at you. *You're* taking this all rather well. The fact that your cat can talk and is practically engaged to an ancient Egyptian goddess doesn't seem to faze you at all."

Valerie had a point. Sabrina wasn't sure what to say or do about it, though. On the one hand, it seemed a bit useless to pretend that she was bowled over by all the magic flowing around them. But on the other, if they got out of this, the less explaining Sabrina had to do about her casual reaction, the better.

So Sabrina shrugged as she pulled on her cornrow wig and checked her appearance in the mirror. "I think I'm in shock," she said. "Everything is so intensely strange that I feel kind of numb, know what I mean?" She frowned. "And I am definitely not made for black hair. Ick."

"I think you look nice," Valerie said loyally. "Kind of like Cleopatra."

"Good, because that was what I was going for," Sabrina quipped. She flopped down on a basket-shaped bed and propped her elbows on her knees. "Valerie, do you think we'll ever see Westbridge again? I'd give anything to be sitting in my backyard, griping about how bored I am."

Valerie smiled wanly. "I think this is the part where Dorothy clicks her shoes together and says, 'There's no place like home.' "

Now Sabrina wished she'd sent them back home when she had the chance. She could have asked her aunts to help her rescue Salem. Now her magic wasn't working, and she had no one to help in restoring it.

"Wait a minute! I sure do!" she cried, leaping off the bed and executing a little jump that sent her wig askew. "The court magician."

Valerie shrugged. "The court magician what? And you sure do what?"

"I sure do have someone I can ask to send us back home." She smiled at Valerie. "Tell you what. I'll go look for him and you hold down the fort."

"What's to hold?" Valerie asked. "Let's go together and find this guy."

Sabrina shook her head. "One of us has to stay here in case our 'master' calls for us."

"And if he does and I'm here all by myself, what do I say?" Valerie asked anxiously. "That you escaped and left me?"

"Valerie, I would do no such thing," Sabrina said, offended. "You're my best friend, in ancient Egypt and in Westbridge. Why would you even think that?"

Valerie made a face. "Because I've been

ditched before, Sabrina. I know the ditching routine from start to finish."

"Well, I'm not ditching you." Sabrina patted her friend's shoulder. "I'm going to see if the court magician will help us."

Valerie clapped her hands. "That's a great idea! Sabrina, you're a genius."

Sabrina grinned. "Just call me Einstein Spellman."

Valerie grinned back. "I'll be waiting. And pacing." She looked around at the vast bedroom. "I wonder how many times around the room equals a mile. I think I remember reading in world history that they measured things in hectares." She cocked her head. "Or was it octaves?"

"I'll be back before you notice I'm gone," Sabrina promised.

That was a promise she very much wanted to keep.

After she shut the door behind herself, she took a deep breath, pointed to herself and murmured a spell of invisibility:

I can walk, and I can run,
But I'm not seen by anyone!

Would her magic work? Then Sabrina tiptoed down a corridor lined with more statues of cats.

"Here goes nothing," she said, with high hopes.

"Here goes nothing," Zelda muttered.

She pointed straight into the air and—*poof!*—she was on the gridiron at Mark Clark College, surrounded by young men in padded football gear, and the ball was sailing straight at her. She cried out, "Don't tackle me!" just as four or five hundred pounds of high school football players pounced.

"Oh, gee, Ms. Spellman," Harvey Kinkle said anxiously. "Guys, guys, get up! This is my girlfriend's aunt."

"Well, she had the ball," another player retorted.

Zelda groaned and said, "Take it, please. It's all yours."

A whistle blew. Harvey said, "Coach has called a time-out." He bent down slightly and frowned with concern at Zelda. "Are you okay?

"Yes, yes," she assured him, secretly pointing to a dozen different places on herself to mend the damage. Without the help of witchcraft, she would have been a mass of bruises and broken bones.

"What are you doing here?" Harvey asked.

"Oh, you know," she said airily. He looked at her expectantly. "Ah, Sabrina's talked about going to school here, and I was antiquing. We need a new dining room table, you know, or rather an old one. . . ." She trailed off, completely out of breath.

"Is Sabrina with you?" he asked excitedly, and Zelda had the answer to the question she didn't want to ask him. Because one of the places on her list that Sabrina might have gone to was this very university, to visit Harvey. Obviously that was not the case.

"Not this trip," she said. "Unfortunately."

"Yeah, most unfortunate," he said. Then he reddened and looked a little shy. "But please tell her I miss her a lot and that when I get home, we'll have a lot of fun."

"I will," Zelda said, feeling even worse. She was beginning to think that this had all started because Sabrina hadn't been having enough fun this summer. If—that is, when—Zelda found her, she would make very sure the rest of Sabrina's vacation was absolutely the most fun she'd ever had in her entire life.

A whistle blew. A man cried, "Let's get back to it, you worms!"

"That's coach," Harvey told her. "He's trying to motivate us with insults."

"What an interesting approach," she replied, smoothing back her hair and tugging on her formerly white linen trousers. "Well, it's been nice seeing you, Harvey."

His brown eyes gleamed. "Same here. I hope

you haven't been maimed for life, being crushed under that pileup."

"Oh, no. Everyone needs at least one football injury to brag about," she assured him.

"Cool." He gave her a little wave as she headed away from the field.

Zelda waved back. Under her breath, she said, "Okay. She's not here. So where is she?"

As Sabrina twisted and turned through the elaborately decorated passageways of the palace, she muttered to herself, "Where am I?"

"It depends on where you want to go," said a familiar voice.

She looked down to see Myron standing directly in her path. The fact that he could see her told her that her magic still wasn't working. That was a very unsettling realization.

"Where have you been?" Sabrina asked.

Myron shrugged. "Your cat's a pretty demanding feline. He asked for a nice soft place to sleep and an endless supply of delightful things to eat. Of course the goddess told me to grant his wishes."

He sighed. "And then she decided I would probably not do a very good job of it, so she sent me to the kitchen to check on the next batch of ankh bread."

"Uh-oh," she said.

"You're speaking my language," he replied. "Well, sorry, but I've got to report back to her."

"Where is Salem?" Sabrina asked.

"Third door past the stone Himalayan Long-hair," he said. "His name was Amenkharis. Nice guy."

He gave her a wave and went on his way.

Sabrina moved on, sneaking down the corridors and peering anxiously around corners.

Then she saw him! The court magician!

He was bustling down a passageway about fifteen feet ahead of her. Darting among the statues, she almost missed the flight of stairs he descended. She heard his footfall on each step.

Breathless, she waited at the top until there were no more sounds. Then she hurried down them as quietly as she could.

At the bottom, almost completely hidden from view by a large palm tree in a planter dotted with cat's-eyes, a small painted wooden door stood ajar. Sabrina wouldn't have noticed it, because it blended in perfectly with the wall painting of a large sphinx staring out over the desert.

Holding her breath, Sabrina gripped the edge of the door and opened it slowly, praying it would not squeak.

The first thing she heard was bubbling, and then the voice of the grand vizier, saying, "And you're certain he doesn't suspect a thing?"

"He is in the dark," the court magician said grandly. His golden cat's-eyes gleamed.

The grand vizier purred. "Excellent."

"Everything is as it should be," said the court magician. "I took his measurements, and I'll finish the Love Mirror of Isis within the hour. When that cat looks into it, on the Night of the Scarab Moon, he will forget everything but the true love of Bast."

Uh-oh.

"What about the girl?" the grand vizier asked. "The witch from the future?"

Big uh-oh.

"It appears that I have successfully blocked her with the mirror." The court magician clapped his hands and raked the air with his claws. "It serves two functions."

What? Sabrina pulled the door open just a tiny crack more. She saw the magician, still in his fancy robes and turban, displaying the mirror to the grand vizier. The faint outline of a figure shimmered in the center of the mirror. Wait a minute! That was a faint outline of her!

"This is her magical persona," the magician said. "The only way she can get it back is to break the mirror."

A gong sounded.

"Hark! Bast is summoning us," the grand vizier announced. "She'll be pleased with your progress."

"Mrrow," the court magician replied.

The two cat-men turned and started for the door.

Yikes!

Sabrina raced up the stairs as fast as she could. She started to take a right toward Salem's room when she heard heavy footfalls just around the corner.

Quickly she flew down the opposite way, weaving this way and that, wishing for all she was worth that she had a trail of invisible bread crumbs to follow.

At last she reached the elaborate door to the bedchamber where she had left Valerie. As she turned the knob, a phalanx of guards trooped down the passage in the direction she had come. In their midst, on a litter covered with pillows, Salem lounged as cat-girls fanned him with palm fronds.

"A little to the left, please," he purred. "Ah, yes, that's much better."

Sabrina darted into their room. Valerie jumped up, her hand still hovering over a tray of tiny decorated cakes. It looked as if she'd eaten about half of them. "I'm so glad you're back! What's going on?"

Sabrina cracked open the door and gestured for Valerie to join her. "Salem's in grave danger," she whispered.

Valerie stood beside her as Salem's entourage

passed them by. "Yeah," Valerie said dryly. "I can see that."

"And so are we," Sabrina added.

Valerie swallowed. "Now *that* I can believe. So what are we going to do?"

"Steal a mirror, ASAP," Sabrina told her. She grabbed Valerie's wrist. "One more thing," she said urgently.

Valerie nodded, wide-eyed. "What?"

Sabrina swallowed hungrily and said, "Are those little cakes any good?"

Chapter 5

When Salem's entourage had passed their quarters, Valerie cocked her head at Sabrina. "Why do we want to steal a mirror? We have a ton of them in our room."

"It's a special mirror," Sabrina said. "It's called the Love Mirror of Isis."

Her mouth was full of cake, which was delicious. Quickly she explained about the love spell, carefully omitting any reference to the fact that her own spell-casting ability was being blocked by the very same mirror.

Valerie made a face. "So once he looks into the mirror, he'll forget about everything but Bast?"

Sabrina nodded.

"Wow." Valerie brightened. "After we steal it,

let's keep it. This really cute guy sits across from me in math and—"

"Valerie," Sabrina remonstrated, "we shouldn't use magic to get what we want."

She hesitated. That wasn't accurate or honest, at least in her case. But no witch was allowed to use magic to make someone fall in love with her. That was against the rules. And Sabrina had learned in the past couple of years that a lot of rules went along with being a witch and using magical powers.

She tried again. "What I mean is—"

"I know, I know. I have to snag him on my own merit." Valerie sighed. "Not for nothing do I live in New England, home of the Puritan work ethic."

Sabrina nodded. "That's the spirit."

"So wish me luck, because I'll need it," Valerie added, looking downcast.

"You don't need luck," Sabrina insisted. "You're great! That math guy will adore you just the way you are."

"Right. Just like he adores me now," Valerie moaned.

Sabrina was frustrated by her friend's lack of self-confidence. In school, kids got divided up into the popular and not-so-popular crowds. Sabrina herself wasn't exactly sure how it happened. She did know, however, that Libby Chessler, the very popular cheerleader, helped keep her and Valerie in the not-so-popular crowd by looking down her nose at them and calling them freaks. Although maybe in Sabrina's case she had a point. After all, Sabrina *was* a witch. . . .

"Well, before we work on that math guy, we need to get back to our own time zone, so let's get to work." Sabrina clapped her hands. She looked around the room and spied two lovely scarves peeking out of a basket, one sky blue and one shocking pink, both decorated with little cat's-eyes outlined with black. "Since we don't have cat faces, we stick out like sore thumbs. Let's disguise ourselves."

Sabrina picked up the blue scarf, draped it over her hair, and covered the lower half of her face with the rest of it. She fastened it in place with a butterfly pin she had been wearing and fluttered her lashes at Valerie.

"Voilà! My disguise."

Valerie nodded. "It works for me." She copied Sabrina's look with the pink scarf and made a little curtsy.

"It works for you, too," Sabrina informed her. "Okay. Let's get going. The mirror is down in the court magician's laboratory."

They sneaked back into the corridor and began to tiptoe past all the cat statues. There certainly were a lot of them.

"This cat goddess goes through more boyfriends than Libby," Sabrina muttered.

"I'll say," Valerie replied. She tapped one. "Wouldn't it be awful to be turned into stone?"

"Yeah. I hear it's pretty rough," Sabrina replied. "I mean, I assume it would be pretty rough."

They returned to the palm tree in front of the hidden door, which had no doorknob and no visible latch. Sabrina hesitated, wishing she could just point at the door and make it open.

"It was open last time," she said. "I don't know how to get inside."

"Maybe . . ." Valerie suggested. She pulled on the fronds of the palm tree, twisting them this way and that. When she tugged on the largest frond, the door opened.

"Woo-hoo," Sabrina said happily. "High five, Valerie!"

They clapped hands.

Sabrina made sure her veil was in place, adjusted Valerie's to throw a shadow over her eyes, and said, "Now all we have to do is find that mirror and break it into a thousand pieces."

Filled with confidence, Sabrina stepped into the laboratory.

The spotless laboratory, where all the workbenches were completely bare.

The laboratory in which there no longer appeared to be a magic mirror.

Sabrina's eyes widened. "Valerie, it's gone,"

she said anxiously. "The Love Mirror of Isis is gone!"

Now what?

Salem nodded at Myron and, with his paw, tapped the pillow on which he lay.

"Now you're getting the hang of it," Salem said. "Good hip action. It's really happening for you."

Myron smiled as he one-two-cha-cha-cha'ed around Salem's room, past the lotus pond stocked with delectable fish, and around the exquisitely decorated litter box. Way around.

"I'm doing it!" Myron cried. "I'm doing the cha-cha!"

"And next is the mambo. And then the tango. And last, but certainly not least, the lambada, the forbidden dance." Salem wiggled his eyebrows up and down.

"And Bas—I mean, the girl I like—she'll be happy that I learned all this, just for her."

Salem nodded. "Girls are just crazy about guys who can dance. Of course, there is no denying that you're a little short."

"That's not a plus?" Myron said anxiously.

"Not a plus," Salem conceded. "But you've got a lot of personality, especially for a *ushabti*. You'll have your mystery woman eating out of your paw—or rather your little clay hand—in no time."

Myron looked skyward and clasped his hands together. "Oh, I hope so. I've worshiped this particular person from afar for centuries. Uh, I mean, for a long, long time. It seems like centuries, it's been so long."

"But you can't let her know that," Salem drawled. "You've got to play hard to get. If she knows you're crazy about her, she'll exploit you."

"Oh." Myron slumped. "So much to learn, so little time."

"Not really." The cat raised his paw. "Let's get back to the dance lesson. Just in case, let's throw the limbo in, too."

"Oh, the limbo!" Myron cried. "I heard she loves to limbo."

"Then you're in luck."

"I must learn everything right away," Myron said. "The Night of the Scarab is fast approaching"—he looked down at his feet of clay—"and I must steal her away from another."

Salem swished the air with his tail. "All's fair in love and war," he said.

The *ushabti* nodded glumly. "So I've heard."

"Look on the bright side," Salem advised. "You'll be able to dance at my wedding"—his face glowed with love—"when I marry the goddess of my dreams."

Myron groaned.

* * *

Sabrina and Valerie reluctantly shut the door to the magician's laboratory and stared at each other beside the giant palm tree.

"We'll have to look all over the palace," Sabrina said.

Valerie nodded.

On tiptoe and holding their breath, the girls reached the stairs. Breathlessly they started up them. Then Valerie tripped on her hem and fell forward, catching herself with her hands.

"Whoops," she said.

"Hark! Who goes there?" someone shouted.

The girls looked at each other. Sabrina gestured for Valerie to follow her back down the stairs and over to the palm tree. She started tugging on all the fronds.

"How did you do it?" she whispered to Valerie.

"Like this."

Valerie pulled the largest frond and the door snapped open.

They ducked back inside the laboratory and the door swung shut.

"I asked you a question," the voice demanded. Whoever the voice belonged to was coming down the stairs!

"Oh, nothing, nothing," came the high-pitched answer from just outside the closed door.

The door flew open. Sabrina and Valerie both jumped back.

It was Myron. And he looked as astonished to see them as they were to see him.

Behind him, a burly man with a huge ax in his hands approached the room. He hadn't spotted the girls—yet.

"This is the court magician's private chamber," the man said. "What business do you have here?"

Myron swallowed hard and looked at the man. "I was um, going to fetch a ball of mummy wrappings for Bast's beloved."

"In the court magician's laboratory?" the guard demanded, looking unconvinced.

Myron nodded vigorously. "Yes. He keeps a nice fresh supply for when he's wrapping things up."

"I don't believe you. I'm going to call for the court magician himself," the guard replied.

In a little voice, the *ushabti* murmured, "Oh, dear."

Sabrina got to work. Ducking behind one of the workbenches, she tore off the hem off her gauzy dress, working all the way around, and fluffed it into a pile. Then she placed it in the center of her palm and jumped up from behind the bench. "Here are those mummy wrapping for my master," she trilled. "The magician left them here, just as he said he would."

"What?" The *ushabti* stared at her. Then he gazed down at the gauze. "Oh, yes. Good. I'll take them to your master right away."

"We'll go with you," Valerie piped up, glancing at Sabrina, who nodded vigorously.

"Yes. Since we're, um, not doing anything else," Sabrina agreed.

"Especially not anything we shouldn't be doing," Valerie added helpfully.

"Very well." The frowning guard stood aside to let the three of them ascend the stairs.

Sabrina scooped Myron up and they quickly reached the landing. The guard trailed behind them, muttering something about calling his superior.

They walked one, two, three doors down from the three stone Himalayan.

Valerie smiled at the guard. "Be seeing ya."

The guard grunted and lumbered away. As soon as he was out of earshot, Myron turned to Sabrina and said, "You probably saved my life." He cocked his head. "What were you doing down there?"

Sabrina shrugged and put him down on the floor. "Oh, just looking around. We've never been in the palace of an immortal cat goddess before, and we thought we'd explore a little."

"What were *you* doing?" Valerie asked the *ushabti*.

He looked down, clearly ill at ease. "I was trying to steal a magic mirror," he confessed.

Sabrina's eyes widened. She gave Valerie a look, warning her not to say anything.

"Oh, really?" Sabrina said innocently. "Imagine that. A magic mirror. How cool."

"But it was gone." He twisted his hands together. "Listen, I've got to tell you the truth. If Salem looks into that mirror, he will be Bast's love slave for eternity. Or until she gets tired of him, whichever comes first. And you can just bet which does come first."

"And then she'll turn him into a statue?" Valerie guessed.

"That's what she does." He shook his head. "Most of the time. But you just never know. He may be her one and only." He sighed and added softly, "But I'm not sure he's her type."

"Love can be such a crazy thing," Sabrina drawled.

Valerie shrugged. "Well, we'll go spring Salem and you can send us back to our own time. Then who cares about the mirror? It's not like we need it for anything else."

"Oh, but you do," Myron began. He looked at Sabrina. "Because they're also holding your magic hostage in it."

"Our magic?" Valerie echoed.

Sabrina cleared her throat and said, "I know all the advances of our civilization must make it *seem* like we're magical, but really, it all boils down to DVD and pagers."

Myron wrinkled his clay forehead until it appeared to be in danger of cracking. "But you—"

"I have a *secret,*" Sabrina said meaningfully. "Um, a secret craving for saltwater taffy." She laughed nervously and tugged on her cornrow wig. "Do you people have saltwater taffy? No? Well, there's another example of the wonders of the future! It's just the best stuff. Isn't it, Valerie?"

Valerie stared at her friend. "Sabrina, I'd say you've been out in the sun too long, except that we've been indoors all day."

"Being cooped up like this is making me crazy," Sabrina said wildly.

"Stress," Valerie said to Myron. "I knew she'd crack sooner or later. It's not every day you find out your cat is a sought-after sex symbol."

"Who can really dance," Myron added woefully. "And sing like a bird."

"Salem can sing?" Sabrina asked, astounded.

"He can dance?" Valerie asked, equally astounded.

"He's quite the ladies' cat," the *ushabti* said. He shrugged. "Which is why I was trying to get that mirror."

He held out his terra-cotta hands. "Okay, I'll come clean with all of it. I've been in love with

Bast for ages. I've done everything to please her. But all she does is boss me around."

"Well," Sabrina said, as tactfully as she could, "you are kind of a pushover."

"Salem has shown me the error of my ways," he continued. "Bast needs a real man. I see that now. That's why she's so in love with Salem."

"Who is a cat," Sabrina pointed out.

But Myron wasn't listening. "I'm going to stand up to her and let her see who's boss. And then I'm going to dance the lambada with her!"

"That always works for me," Sabrina said, grinning at Valerie. "A bossy boy with rhythm. That's my dream date."

The *ushabti* was lost in his own fantasy as he began to dance around their ankles. "I've got to get him away from her. If he's gone, she'll turn to me. I'll make her so happy. We'll go on a cruise down the Nile. And I'll teach her how to play the sacred game of bingo."

"Which Salem taught you," Sabrina guessed. "You didn't play for money, did you?"

He shook his head. "No. Prizes. I lost a couple of bracelets, but they were too big for me anyway." He shrugged. "That rule where you have to give the other person the chance to call bingo first got me every time."

Sabrina narrowed her eyes. "Call bingo first?"

"Yes." He was very earnest. "You know. When you have a bingo, but you wait for the count of three before you yell it out, so the other guy has a chance to say it."

"Oh, brother." Sabrina shook her head. "Listen, Myron, I'll get your bracelets back for you before we leave."

"No, it's all right," Myron assured her. "He won them fair and square."

Valerie clapped her palm over her forehead. "He sings, he dances, and he cheats at bingo. Is there no limit to what that cat can do?"

Boring.
*Bo*ring, bo*ring,* borrrrrrrring.

Seated at her place among the other witches stuck with council duty, Hilda fought back a yawn as the young warlock with the shaved head and the stud in his nose held out his hands and said, "Honest, I did not know that I was going four thousand miles an hour. My vacuum cleaner's speedometer must be broken."

"That's a misdemeanor in itself," announced the council head, a middle-aged witch in a curly white wig. "The penalty is one week's suspension of all magical powers."

"No, wait!" the young warlock protested. "I was just trying to keep up with the flow of traffic."

The council head looked down her nose at him. "Said flow of traffic was a meteor shower, was it not?"

He grimaced. "Well, yeah, but—"

Hilda finally yawned. She had never endured duller Witches' Council duty. Speeding. Casting spells for profit. Where were the really juicy cases? Why didn't someone try to take over the world, the way Salem used to?

"Ms. Spellman, do you mind?" the council head demanded, and then she, too, yawned. Covering her mouth, she slammed down her gavel and said, "All right. Enough. One week's suspension of powers for speeding, one week for trying to fool your elders, and another week because you're about to say—"

"Oh, *man*," the warlock protested.

"'Oh, *man*,'" the council head mimicked, "which I hate and which is inaccurate, as I am not a man."

Hilda smirked at the warlock as he stomped unhappily away. *Another one bites the dust.*

This council was ruthless. There was a little bit of pleasure to be taken in that.

Then the council bailiff announced, "Next case. Disorderly conduct."

Ho-hum. Hilda studied her nails. It was time to give herself a manicure. She pointed at her left hand, then her right. Her stubby nails became long, oval, and painted with a nice shade of berry.

Much better.

The bailiff continued, "Suspect's name: Ms. Zelda Spellman."

Hilda choked and blurted out, "What?"

Her white linen pants smudged, her face covered with mud, Zelda stepped forward and said, "May I please address the council?" She held her hands out to her sister.

"Hilda, Sabrina's missing."

While Myron kept watch in the hallway, Valerie and Sabrina tiptoed into Salem's room. It was very dark. What Sabrina wouldn't give to be able to light one of her fingertips. But that was not to be until they found the Love Mirror of Isis and destroyed it.

"Look, there's a lump in his bed," Valerie whispered. "It's got to be Salem."

"I dunno," Sabrina whispered back. "There's no snoring."

"He snores, too?" Valerie asked, astonished. "Sabrina, when we get home, you have to call *Sightings*. I swear, Salem's got to be an alien."

"Close," Sabrina muttered. She crept toward the lump. "Salem? Is that you? Wake up. It's Sabrina."

The lump moved.

"Salem?" she tried again, prodding him.

"Huh? Mmmf? Who's there? Guards!" Salem shouted as he awoke from a deep sleep and a bad dream. "I'm being assassinated!"

"Oh, not now!" Sabrina wailed.

From the corridor came Myron's shout, "Oh, my goodness! What can be the matter? All these guards! I just don't know what can be happening!"

And then his voice was drowned out by the clatter and clang of metal on metal and heavy, running feet.

Sabrina grabbed Salem and said, "Cover for us, Salem. If you don't, we're in big trouble!"

"Huh? What?" Salem blinked. "What's going on?"

"Salem," Sabrina said frantically. "You were dreaming about being assassinated. You called for the guards, and they're coming."

"Guards?" His eyes were heavy and muzzy. "Huh. One minute I'm about to take the fort, the next, I—"

There was loud pounding on the door. "Open this door at once!" someone bellowed on the other side.

"Don't shoot!" Valerie cried, raising her hands. "We surrender!"

"We do not surrender," Sabrina said quickly. "We're the ones who saved Salem, aren't we?" She nudged Salem. "Aren't we?"

"Hmm," Salem whispered to her. "This could be interesting. What's it worth to you?"

"Salem, come on. Remember, I turned you over while you were tanning," Sabrina said under her breath. "And who got you lift tickets for Christmas?"

"What?" Valerie squealed. *"Lift tickets?"*

"Hey, I helped pick out your present," Salem said to her. "That sweater was very nice." He preened. "The lift tickets were better. But then, I'm family."

Valerie tried again. To Sabrina she said, "You bought your cat *ski lift tickets?"*

"I can't exactly walk up the slopes," he retorted.

The door burst open.

"Death to the assassins!" one of the guards shouted, as some men carried torches into the room. "Slay them immediately."

The guards surrounded the bed and aimed their swords and spears directly at Valerie and Sabrina.

"Salem, say something!" Sabrina cried.

Salem flicked his tail. *"Meow?"*

☆

Chapter 6

☆

"Okay, okay, hold your horses—or rather your spears," Salem said to the guards as they pointed their weapons at Sabrina and Valerie. "It's true. My handmaidens did save me."

He flicked his tail at Sabrina. "There. Happy now?"

"I must be dreaming," Valerie murmured to herself. "Sabrina bought her cat lift tickets for Christmas."

"Oh, dear, oh dear," Myron said, easing his way through the crowd. "Excuse me, yes, you— **the** one with the huge sword and the very big **feet**. Pardon me."

He looked up at Sabrina and said loudly, "Wow, good thing you rescued Salem."

"What did the assassins look like?" one of the guards asked Sabrina. He replaced his sword on his belt and pulled out a piece of papyrus and a quill. "I'll need a full description."

"They looked like cat-people," Sabrina said, figuring that was a vague enough description to avoid getting anyone in trouble.

The guard looked over his shoulder at the others. A few of them nodded. "It's got to be the Amenhotep Gang." To Sabrina he said, "We've been after them for months. Unruly alley-cat types. They yowl at the moon, dig in trash cans. We caught a couple of them hacking up fur balls and making prank catcalls out by the pyramids. I'm sure you know the type."

Sabrina glanced archly at Salem. "Oh, yes," she said, amused. "I know the type pretty well."

"Hey." Salem sounded highly insulted. "I do not *yowl*. I have perfect pitch."

"Make way for the goddess!" someone cried.

Trumpets blared. Cymbals clanged. Salem's eyes gleamed. "It's her," he said dreamily.

"That should be, 'It's she,'" Myron corrected him. "'She' is a nominative-case pronoun whereas 'her'—"

"Oh, Myron, do be quiet," Bast said, as she swept regally into the room. Everyone in the place fell to the floor at once—except Valerie. Sabrina tugged on her hand and she plopped down next to her.

"Salem-hotep, I came as quickly as I could," Bast said, picking Salem up and hugging him. "I heard about the attempt on your life. I was so worried about you!"

Sabrina and Valerie traded looks. *Salem-hotep?*

Salem thrust forward his lower lip. "I'm all right now, but it was a harrowing experience. Apparently they were going to hold me for ransom, which they expected you to pay. In fish heads."

Bast stroked his back. "Ah, my love. I would give them every fish head in the two kingdoms to ensure your safe return. I will never, ever part with you, not for nine lifetimes!"

"Oh, great," Valerie whispered to Sabrina, who elbowed her to be quiet.

"They wanted chocolate chip cookies, too," Salem added innocently. "Dozens of them."

"Chocolate chip cookies? This is something I have not heard of," the goddess said, a trifle concerned.

"Highness, they are from the future," Myron informed her, stepping forward and bowing. "I can give you the recipe, or, better yet, make them myself."

"Silence!" Bast thundered. "You will speak only when spoken to."

The *ushabti* put his hands on his hips and stomped his foot. "Now, see here—" he began.

The golden woman whirled on him. *"What?"*

Sabrina stepped forward. "See here," she said, pointing to the floor. "There's a . . . um . . . Valerie, did you see that big poison scorpion skitter across the floor?"

The guards all gave a shout. Myron leaped into Sabrina's hands and cried, "Where? Where? A little guy like me, I've got to be careful. If one of those things bites me, I'm ancient history. Well, actually I already *am* ancient history."

"You're also made out of clay," Sabrina pointed out. "So I doubt a scorpion bite would do you much harm."

Bast rolled her eyes. "Myron, you are so spineless." She clapped her hands. "Guards, find the scorpion!"

Then she smiled at Sabrina and Valerie. "You saved my beloved's life—perhaps twice, with your warning about the scorpion. You truly are his friends. You will be my special guests at the banquet." She beamed at Salem. "Soon it will be the Night of the Scarab, and this exquisite tomcat and I will celebrate the joining of our hearts in eternal love."

"Cool," Sabrina said unenthusiastically.

Valerie piped up, "What should we wear?"

"Special garments will be provided for you," Bast told her, "as befits your station."

Salem sighed and smiled up at Bast. "Isn't this goddess just the greatest?" he asked.

"Absolutely," Myron said adoringly.

Bast glared at the statuette. "I told you to be silent!"

"Right, right," Myron mumbled, bowing and scraping. "So very sorry, Your Glory."

"Salem-hotep, my darling, let's walk by the lotus pond," Bast said to Salem. "I need to recover from the fear of losing you."

"Your wish is my command," Salem replied.

"Oh, you are so wonderful," Bast gushed.

They left together.

"How come when *he* says stuff like that, she thinks it's wonderful?" Myron grumbled. "But when *I* say stuff like that, I'm a wimp?"

"I can't help you there," Sabrina said. "I'm just as confused as you are."

She looked at Valerie and Myron. "We're going to have to work out a plan to stop Salem from looking in that mirror tomorrow night."

"We could have a piñata," the *ushabti* suggested, "and make him wear a blindfold. Then we'll get him to break the mirror by accident." He made a face. "Of course, Bast will probably turn the three of you to stone as a result. But there's always a chance she'll turn you back once she calms down."

"Oh," Valerie said. "That's nice to know."

"Yeah. Except that it will take her a century or two to calm down," he went on.

"Or not so nice," Sabrina said. "I guess it's back to the drawing board."

"Back to the drawing board," Valerie concurred.

The *ushabti* said, "What's a drawing board?"

Hilda and Zelda faced the Witches' Council as the head witch finished faxing the group's lunch order to the Other Realm Deli and Bakery ("You Wish It, We Dish It"). The order arrived two milliseconds later, and all of the councillors tucked into their pastrami on rye.

All of them except Hilda and Zelda, that is. They were too worried to eat.

"And I haven't been able to find Sabrina anywhere," Zelda was saying to the council.

"You've barely looked," the head of the council retorted as she chomped on her dill pickle. "I've had fairy-tale characters in here who could find a needle in a haystack. You can't find one niece in the mortal realm?"

"She has a point," Hilda said.

"Whose side are you on, Hildy?" Zelda demanded. "I went to a lot of trouble to get arrested just so I could talk to you."

It was true; she had started a riot at the Other Realm House of Pizzazz by saying in a loud voice, "Can it be true? Everything is fifty percent off for the next two minutes?"

"Yes, but you also got some great bargains," Hilda shot back.

"Ladies, ladies," the council head said wearily, "can we please get back to the matter at hand, which is the fact that you have lost your niece?" She picked up her sandwich bag. "And my sandwich came with ranch-flavored chips. They are now missing. Did someone swipe them?"

"We didn't lose her," Zelda said defensively. "We simply don't know where she is. Like your chips."

"Here, Your Honor," said a witch dressed in a medieval-princess cone hat. She held up a bag of chips. "They accidentally put two bags in with my order."

The council head took them and ripped open the bag. She selected a chip from the bag and munched on it thoughtfully. "Stale," she announced. "For the record, we're fining the deli within an inch of their lives."

"But, Your Honor, their pickles are delicious. They more than make up for the stale chips," the cone-headed princess said.

"True. All right. They're on probation." She smiled at the princess. "You have a great future ahead of you in the legal profession. Now listen, you two," she said, pointing her gavel at Hilda and Zelda. "If Sabrina were a pair of glasses, she would be considered lost." She slammed down her gavel. "I hereby order you to find your niece within twenty-four hours, or I will turn both of you into pairs of glasses!"

"Hey, our cat got a lighter punishment for trying to take over the world," Hilda protested.

"He's not *your* cat. Cats never belong to anybody," the council head declared. "That's my judicial pronouncement."

"So I'm excused to help look for Sabrina?" Hilda asked hopefully.

"I suppose so," the council head said irritably. She glared at the bailiff. "Who's our first alternate for council duty?"

The bailiff clapped his hands and said, "Vesta Spellman, come on down!"

Poof! Vesta appeared in a jet-black judge's robe studded with diamonds at the collar and hem. And speaking of the hem, it barely reached her knees, unlike the usual ankle-length garment. She also wore an amazing white wig trimmed with black ostrich feathers.

"Here I am," Judge Vesta said, voguing. "I say we let everybody off with a warning today. Wouldn't that be nice?"

"Vesta, you are not the judge," said the head of the council. "And please zap yourself up something more appropriate to wear."

Vesta glanced at Hilda and Zelda and did a

double take at Zelda's appearance. "Something more appropriate for what? Mud wrestling? Zelda, what on earth happened to you?"

Zelda tried to wipe the dirt off her face as she waved a hand at Vesta. "It's not important. What is important is that we can't find Sabrina."

"Or Salem," Hilda added.

"Or Sabrina's mortal friend, Valerie," Zelda added uncomfortably.

"Oh, dear, this is serious," Vesta murmured. As she pointed herself out of her judicial robes and into a nicely flared black skirt and a black turtleneck sweater, she turned to the head of the council. "Surely I can be excused from duty to help my sisters look for our niece?"

The head of the council rolled her eyes and sighed. "Is this some kind of conspiracy among you Spellmans to get out of your service to the council?"

"Absolutely not," Hilda assured her, but she did find herself thinking it was neat that things were turning out that way.

Zelda stepped forward. "And to prove it, Hilda will resume her duty as soon as Sabrina is located. In fact, she'll serve for an extra week!"

"Hey," Hilda protested.

"Done!" said the head of the council, as she slammed her gavel down.

"Wait," Hilda squawked.

"Not now, Hildy," Zelda said under her breath. "We've got to get out of here and find Sabrina."

"That's for sure," Hilda muttered back. "If we stick around any longer, you'll probably volunteer me for two more weeks of council duty."

"Done!" said the head of the council.

Hilda groaned.

Bast's entire palace was abuzz with excitement as everyone prepared for the great feast of the Night of the Scarab. The palace servants scoured the place from top to bottom. All the cat-people preened and groomed themselves. Sabrina and Valerie received long gauzy slip dresses that looked a lot like their first raiment. They each also got fancy new wigs, jewelry, and a small vial of perfume, which they daubed on.

The goddess went around humming the Egyptian wedding march.

And Salem, despite his pleads and protests, had a bath.

Sabrina couldn't help laughing when Myron told her about it.

"He kept saying he was allergic to water, but no one would listen," Myron said. "Now he's lying in the sun, sulking."

Sabrina's ears perked up. "Alone?"

Myron shrugged. "Last I saw."

"Woo-hoo!" Sabrina cried. "Myron, this is our chance to tell him what's going on. Then we'll get out of here and go back to Westbridge!"

He held up his hand. "Don't forget, I'm a cat pleaser. I can send him back only if he wants to go. Otherwise I'm powerless."

Sabrina shrugged. "Well, all we can do is try."

"And fail," Valerie said gloomily.

Sabrina gave her a mock punch in the arm. "Don't be so pessimistic. I'm sure Salem's bored with this place already."

Boredom was fine with him, though, she realized nervously, remembering how Salem had no trouble back home with having nothing to do all day but get a sun tan. He loved boredom. He lived for it.

"Yeah," Valerie said as the three walked down one of the many statue-lined corridors of the palace. "His every whim seen to, his favorite foods prepared and served on fancy dishes by cat-girls. I can certainly see why he'd be eager to leave," she observed, her tone sarcastic.

Myron, riding on Sabrina's shoulder, held up a small clay hand. "Don't forget the bath. He did not like the bath."

"My aunt bathes him once a week, whether he needs it or not," Sabrina pointed out. "That's not much of an improvement over here."

"Speaking of beauty secrets," Myron said,

"what's that perfume you're wearing, Sabrina? I love it!"

"Thanks. It was in our room," Sabrina said. "It's called Simply Irresistible."

"Ah. Simply Irresistible. It's supposed to make you—guess what?—irresistible." He grinned at Sabrina. "I'm not a good test case, since I'm a clay figurine, but it's got my vote."

"I have some on, too," Valerie said glumly. "Don't you smell it?"

"I'm on Sabrina's shoulder," the *ushabti* reminded her. "But, yes, now that you mention it, I can detect a subtle fragrance. Get within range of any young Egyptian guys, and you two girls will have dates for the big feast!"

Sabrina gave her cornrow wig a shake. "Myron, remember, we don't want to be here for the feast. We want to be home."

"Yes, with our perfume on," Valerie said eagerly. "Just in time for math class."

"Math," Myron said, shaking his head. "It's the shortest class we have here. On account of we haven't invented the concept of zero yet. It's very difficult to calculate much of anything without the zero."

Then he tapped Sabrina on the shoulder. "Look. There's Salem-hotep."

In a small courtyard beyond several statues of Manx cats, Salem held court beside a large pond dotted with lotuses. Sabrina slumped with frustration. He was was not alone. Catching the rays of Ra, the sun god, he was lounging on a velvet hammock in the sun, one cat-girl fanning him slowly with a palm frond, another one feeding him grapes, and a third giving him a pawdicure. His eyes were shut and he was sighing with pleasure.

The trio approached him. A couple of cat-servants rushed forward with little backless chairs, and Sabrina and Valerie sat on them. The sun beat down, and Sabrina thought wistfully of the oven timer, and how distraught it would be that she had on no sunscreen.

"Hi, Salem. Hotep," Sabrina added, as he opened one lazy eye at her. "How are you doing?"

"Terrific." He sighed again. "Isn't this the most wonderful place, Sabrina? I can't believe our good fortune. And to think I almost spent the duration of my sentence as a cat in Westbridge. I shudder when I think about how close I came to missing all this."

Sabrina made a face at Valerie and Myron, who made faces back at her.

"Yes, well . . ." She hesitated, not sure how to proceed. "Don't you think it's time to go home?"

"Sabrina, I *am* home," Salem said. He rolled

on his back as the cat-girl with the grapes popped another succulent morsel into his mouth. Then she daubed his whiskers with a little cloth and he sighed with contentment.

"Don't you remember the winters in Westbridge?" he went on, stretching. "The snow, the sleet, the long gray afternoons? They don't have those here. Egypt enjoys an endless summer."

He raised his right forepaw and examined his pawdicure. His nails were buffed to a gleam. He murmured, "Wow, I can see myself. And I look *good.*"

"Salem-hotel," Valerie said.

"Hotep," Salem corrected her, yawning.

"Okay. Sorry. I'm not good at last names. But you've got to listen to Sabrina." She gestured to his entourage and to their surroundings, then held out her hands. "Sure, this place looks cool, but staying here would be like—oh, I don't know—like living at the mall." Valerie blinked. "Which I would do, actually, if I could. There's absolutely no downside to that."

She shrugged apologetically and turned to her friend. "Sorry, Sabrina. I guess I'm no good at this. After all, Salem has a point. Back home he's just a cat. I think."

Sabrina sighed and took over. "Salem-hotep, I need to speak with you privately," Sabrina said.

Salem yawned. "Sabrina, anything you want

to say to me, you can say to these lovelies. They're my people." He smiled at the cat-girls. "Right, ladies?"

"Mrrow, master," they said in unison.

"Master," Salem murmured. "I never get tired of hearing that. And it's better than the old days, Sabrina. Here, I get to be ruler without even fighting a single battle. Isn't that terrific?"

Valerie frowned. "What is he talking about?"

"I think he has a touch of sunstroke," Sabrina said. She decided to try again. "Well, yes, Salem-hotep, except for one thing." She sighed. "Um, your girlfriend's kind of, ah, she's—"

"On her way here now," Valerie said nervously. She jumped out of her chair. "And oh, I'm freckling. Time to get out of this harsh Egyptian sun."

"I hear you," Sabrina said, as she leaped of her chair with Myron in hand.

The three of them hurried away and hid behind a column just as Bast glided to Salem's side. In the sun, she looked even more goddesslike, glowing and golden. And very much in love.

"Well, that was a bust," Sabrina muttered.

"What did I tell you?" Valerie said.

"Oh, no, look." Sabrina pointed to the morsel of ankh bread that the goddess was feeding Salem.

Valerie groaned. "Two down. One to go."

"We've got to do something." Sabrina

scratched her cheek. "If Salem looks in the mirror tonight, he's lost. And so are we."

"She's lost. And so are we," Vesta said. She pointed a map into existence, then impatiently waved her fingers so that the map was hovering right side up. "I thought you said her friend Libby was somewhere in France."

The three witches stared at the scene before them. Half a dozen men in dark clothes and square, wide-brimmed hats were tilling fields with the aid of horses drawing old-fashioned plows. A woman in a bonnet and a plain gray-and-black dress was pouring lemonade at a wooden picnic table.

"I think this is a different France," Hilda said slowly. "Like maybe somewhere in Pennsylvania. Zeldy, these people are Amish."

"Oh." Vesta frowned. "They're not usually found in the South of France."

"No, but they make beautiful quilts," Zelda said eagerly. "Perhaps we could—"

"Come back later," Hilda said meaningfully. "Like when I'm on my *extra* Witches' Council duty."

Zelda sighed. "All right."

Vesta pointed and said:

> *Let's all sing and let's all dance.*
> *Let's all go to ooh-la-la France!*

Poof!

Zelda, Hilda, and Vesta stood on a beach, every other square inch of which was crowded with sunbathers in bikinis, swim trunks, or Speedos. The sun worshipers, slathered with suntan lotion, were dozing in beach chairs, chatting with each other, reading, and listening to music through earphones.

"Wow, good thing our kitchen timer isn't here," Hilda said. "It would be passing out leaflets about skin cancer by now."

"Oh, my goodness," Vesta gasped, as a very handsome man sauntered by. "This is a wonderful place."

Zelda wagged her finger at her sister. "Now, now, Vesta. We're supposed to be looking for Sabrina's friend Libby. Well, she's not her friend, exactly. In fact, Sabrina can't stand her. They don't get along at all."

"So why would Sabrina come to see her in France?" Hilda pressed, pointing herself into a tropical floral bathing suit and a matching floppy hat. "And are you two interested in boogie boarding?"

"Hilda, we don't have time to enjoy ourselves," Zelda chided her.

Vesta pointed herself into a bikini and a parasol and said, "Zelda, dressing for the occasion won't hurt our search. And as for enjoying ourselves . . ." She pointed again and a handsome, tanned blond man in swimming trunks appeared at her side.

"Who is that?" Zelda demanded.

"I am Jean-Michel," he said, in a thick foreign accent. "At your servees, mademoiselle."

"I'm accessorizing," Vesta said, grinning. She slipped her arm through Jean-Michel's. "Come on, darling. Help us look for Libby."

To Zelda's amazement, the man raised a hand and pointed dead ahead. "Dere she is," he announced.

Indeed, Sabrina's high school nemesis, was wedged between her parents on the crowded beach. Her father was talking on a cell phone, and her mother held a sun reflector beneath her chin. Libby stared grumpily at a magazine. All three were wearing sunglasses.

"I don't see Sabrina with them," Hilda said uncertainly.

"But Libby might know where she is," Zelda pointed out. "We need to look everywhere. Leave no stone unturned."

"Yeah, or we're going to be eyeglasses," Hilda grumbled.

They made a little parade as they walked through the sand, Zelda in the lead, followed by Hilda, then Vesta, then Jean-Michel, who held Vesta's parasol over her head. A few sunbathers complained as they briefly blocked out the sun. But these were witches on a mission, and they marched on ahead without a moment's hesitation.

At last they reached Libby's striped beach towel. Zelda feigned surprise and called out, "Libby Chessler? It can't be!"

Libby lowered her magazine—*Young and Wealthy*—and pulled her sunglasses down her nose. Her eyebrows shot up and she said, "No. Please. Don't tell me Sabrina's here!"

"Okay, we won't." Zelda looked at Hilda, who looked at Vesta, who looked at Jean-Michel.

"And so we assume you haven't seen her in, oh, say, the past three days," Hilda ventured.

"No way." Libby made a face. Then she frowned at them. "But if *you're* here . . ."

"Sabrina's not," Hilda said. She shrugged. "She's not a beach person, I guess."

"Oh. Good." Libby lay back down.

"Who are these people, darling?" Libby's mother asked in a snobbish tone of voice.

"People who were just leaving," Zelda filled in, gesturing for the others to follow her and walk away.

As they did so, Vesta said, "Did you see her mother's earrings? Canary diamonds to die for! That family must be very rich."

"Rich in money, but not in much else," Zelda told her. "Actually, we've always felt a little sorry for Libby, despite the grief she occasionally causes Sabrina."

Vesta shielded her gaze and looked out over the vast beach. "Well, I don't think Sabrina's here," she said. "So now what?"

Hilda and Zelda looked at each other and shrugged.

Jean-Michel said, "Anyone for *le* volleyball?"

Chapter 7

☆

Well, it's time for the feast," Sabrina said unhappily as she and Valerie readjusted their heavy wigs in their room.

"Time to admit defeat," Myron chimed in. He had added a fresh coat of glaze to himself for the big night, and now he shone as if he had on sparkly body lotion.

"Hey, wait a minute." Sabrina folded her arms. "We are not quitters! There has to be a way to stop Salem from gazing into the mirror."

"We could try a highly charged game of Simon Says," Valerie suggested.

Sabrina paced. "We've tried to reason with him. The only solution is to get the mirror."

"We could kidnap the court magician," Valerie piped up.

"Hey," Sabrina said excitedly. "That's a good idea!"

Myron waved his hands. "No, no, no. *Bad* idea. Very bad. If you think Bast's a heap of trouble, try tangling with Harry Houdini–hotep there."

"Who's Harry Houdini?" Valerie and Sabrina asked in unison.

"Houdini was a famous magician of just before your time," Myron explained. "Or rather, close to your time. But I guess not close enough." He glanced at Sabrina. "I thought you might know who is he, on account of you are a wit—"

"A witless student of American history," Sabrina finished nervously. She laughed shrilly. "Those pesky dates. Who can keep them straight?"

Truth be told, Sabrina knew she was way overdue to explain to the *ushabti* that her being a witch and having magical powers was a big secret, which she had not shared with Valerie. Well, not on a permanent basis or in a way that Valerie could remember.

Sabrina thought he would have figured that out by now, but obviously he hadn't. She wasn't supposed to let any mortal know that she was a witch. That was one of the most important rules she had to follow as a witch living in the mortal realm.

She also needed to ask Myron if there was another way to regain her powers besides getting hold of the Love Mirror of Isis. But so far she hadn't had a chance to speak to him privately about either of these things since they'd become allies in their attempt to keep Salem from becoming Mr. Bast number one hundred kabillion seventeen zillion and one.

Sabrina figured she was exaggerating only slightly, because there were stone cat statues *everywhere* in Bast's palace!

A loud gong clanged. Valerie cried out in surprise and grabbed Sabrina.

"It's suppertime," Myron said unhappily. "Time for the big feast where Bast feeds your cat the third piece of ankh bread and gets him to gaze into the Love Mirror of Isis."

Sadly he gestured for the girls to follow him. "Some animals have all the luck," he muttered.

Sabrina scooped him up and carried him on her shoulder as they hurried through the halls. " Myron, I don't get it," she told him. "You know Bast is fickle. Look at all the husbands she's had! Why do you want her to fall in love with you?"

He held out his hands, then touched his heart. "How do you explain love?" he asked. He sniffed the air. "You're both wearing Simply Irresistible, aren't you?"

"Yeah. But obviously we aren't," Valerie said. "Irresistible, that is."

"Do you really want to be irresistible around here?" Sabrina asked her. "Our boyfriends would have whiskers."

"Well, the guy in my math class *has* been trying to grow a goatee," Valerie said dreamily. "I noticed the stubble on his chin."

"See? Now, why can't Bast notice my goatee?" Myron asked petulantly. "I've had this thing for, oh, at least ten thousand years."

"Love is blind, I guess," Sabrina said. She couldn't help chuckling.

"It's not funny," Myron grumped, from where he sat on Sabrina's shoulders. He crossed his legs and leaned his chin on his elbows. "I'm really suffering."

Sabrina gave his head a pat. "Well, we'll do our best to get Salem out of the picture." And back to Westbridge. Sabrina couldn't wait to get home.

The gong sounded again. Myron tapped Sabrina's shoulder.

"Better hurry," he said. "If we're late . . ." He made a slicing motion across his neck.

"You're kidding, right?" Valerie asked anxiously.

Just then an enormous lionlike guard wheeled around the corner. He was carrying an equally enormous ax over his shoulder.

"Gulp. Guess not," Valerie murmured. She smiled and waved at the guard. "Hi. How's everything?"

"Just ducky," he replied, scowling. "Everybody else gets to go to the feast, but *I* have to guard the Love Mirror of Isis."

Sabrina nearly choked and Valerie froze in astonishment. Sabrina collided with her. Myron soared into the air and landed with a crash on the marble floor.

Where he split in half from the center of his forehead down the length of his torso.

"Oh, Myron!" Sabrina cried. She ran to him and picked him up, one half in each hand.

"Goo," he panted. "Goo."

"What?" Sabrina asked each half in turn. "What are you saying?"

"Sabrina, the guard's getting away!" Valerie cried.

"Oh, no!" Sabrina moaned.

Quickly she pressed the two halves of Myron together. He said immediately, "Gah-lue! Get me some glue!"

Sabrina nodded vigorously, "Oh, okay. Glue. Don't worry. We'll get glue!"

Anxiously she looked up.

The guard was gone.

And so was Valerie.

"Go, Valerie," Sabrina said.

"Glue, glue," Myron urged.

Sabrina ran to where they had encountered the guard, but the hall was empty.

Then the gong sounded again. Suddenly the corridor was filled with cat-people. They spilled out the doors and into the halls. All of them were dressed in fancy robes, their eyes lined with black pencil. They were chattering excitedly, their conversations punctuated with meows.

"I give this marriage two weeks," one tabby-like cat-guy said.

"Nine days," another answered.

"You're on." They high-fived each other.

"Oh, dear," Sabrina murmured, as she and the *ushabti* were caught up in the swirl. Then she raised her voice and asked, "Excuse me. Does anybody have some glue?"

"There should be some in the guard room," said the tabby guy. He pointed to the left. "It's just a paw's throw from here. Go down that corridor. When you get to the golden statue of our goddess, hang a left."

"Oh. Thanks," Sabrina said.

"Mrrrow," he replied.

Sabrina followed his directions. Soon she was standing in front of a door that read Guards Only. No Admittance.

She swallowed and said, "No admittance."

Myron groaned.

Sabrina fitted his two halves together so that

he could speak. "Please, just ask for some glue," he said. "I have a splitting headache!"

Swallowing, she rapped on the door. "Hello?" she called out. "I'm sorry to bother you, but—"

The door opened. A figure her height—in other words, a bit on the short side, for a guard—yanked the door open. Though it carried a spear and a shield, it was covered from head to toe in white cotton robes. A large sash was wrapped over its nose, and the front of its headdress draped over its eyes.

It said gruffly, "Yes?"

"We're looking for glue," Sabrina said breathlessly. "I accidentally broke this guy, and—"

The guard leaned forward and drew the cotton drapes from around its mouth.

"Sabrina, it's me, Valerie," she whispered.

"Val, what are you doing in there?" she whispered back.

"You'll never guess." Valerie's eyes were shining.

"You're right. Tell me," Sabrina urged.

Valerie grinned at her. "Guess."

"Oh, Valerie, please! Just tell me."

Valerie took a step to one side.

Sabrina stared at herself, perfectly reflected in the elaborately framed mirror. The mirror with the golden cats decorating the rim.

"The Love Mirror of Isis," Sabrina breathed.

Then she saw a blurred double of her silhouette waving behind her reflection. She knew it must be her magical persona!

"Val, how did you get it?" Sabrina said, excited. "All we have to do is—"

"I don't exactly have it," Valerie replied.

"What is this girl doing here?" demanded a resounding voice.

The same tall, burly lion-guard Sabrina and Valerie had just encountered strode up behind Valerie, still carrying his weapon and still looking fierce and impatient.

Valerie covered her features as fast as she could. Then she cleared her throat. The next time she spoke, it was in a low, masculine voice, something like the one Sabrina had had when she'd turned herself in a boy for a couple of days.

"She's looking for—"

"Glue," Sabrina said with a big, nervous grin. "I dropped Salem-hotep's *ushabti* and I want to make sure he's in good order and able to serve Salem-hotep during the big feast."

"Mmm." The guard cocked his head. "If the goddess knew of this, she would scratch your eyes out."

"Oh, um," Sabrina said anxiously, "we wouldn't want that, would we?"

The guard slammed a hand down on Valerie's shoulder. Valerie buckled beneath the man's hand but somehow managed to stay on her feet.

"Absolutely not. No one wants Bast displeased. Find this girl some glue."

Valerie scurried off.

Sabrina pointed to the mirror. "That's some mirror," she said.

"Yes." The guard looked proud. "We've been assigned to guard it until dessert. Then we'll take it into the throne room."

"Oh," Sabrina squeaked. "Not until dessert?"

The man nodded. "Candied catnip leaves will be served in approximately five hours."

"What?" Sabrina cried. "Five hours?"

The man shrugged. "We're Egyptians. We like to party." He sniffed. "Hmm, what's that you're wearing?"

"Here's the glue," Valerie announced in her deep voice.

She held out an earthenware jar. As Sabrina took it, she saw that there was a note attached to it. Eagerly she palmed it and said, "Gee, thanks. I'll return it later."

"Uh-uh-uh," the man said, wagging his finger. "Just take it over there and use it. Let him know when you're finished." He slammed his hand down on Valerie's shoulder again. Valerie staggered again.

The man tromped away. Sabrina unfastened the note and read it: "The magician just came by. He said the mirror is ready to go. He also said you and I will be stuck here for all time once Salem looks into it!"

"That's not good news," Sabrina whispered, "unless you factor in that we won't have to do homework ever again." She smiled weakly.

In reply Valerie stamped her foot.

"I didn't figure you would think that was funny," Sabrina said.

Valerie followed Sabrina as she carried Myron and the jar over to a small table. Across the room, cat-men were pulling out handfuls of coins.

"I give the cat *seven* days before Bast turns him to stone," one of them was saying.

"I shouldn't even bet," another one drawled. "I have inside information that he has fleas. You know how Bast hates that."

"He does not—" Sabrina began, then shut her mouth as Valerie gestured for her to be quiet.

Sabrina sighed and swabbed glue all over one side of Myron, and then over the other. She pressed the two halves together. He exhaled with relief.

"Thank you," he said, massaging his forehead. "Y'know, the last girl who dropped me only broke my heart. Ba-dum-dum."

"Sssh," Sabrina cautioned. "We're in the guard room."

"Right. Right." He jerked his head in the

direction of the mirror. "Now all we have to do is steal that thing and—"

"All finished?" the burly guard asked Sabrina.

"Um, yes. So I, uh—"

"That's great." He slammed his hand down on Valerie's shoulder again. "Escort the great-smelling maiden and the *ushabti* out." He paused. "Soldier, are you wearing perfume?"

Valerie shook her head and practically dragged Sabrina and Myron into the hall.

"What now?" Valerie whispered.

"You have to try to grab the mirror," Sabrina whispered.

Valerie shook her head. "No way. They'd kill me. Someone's bound to figure out that I don't belong in there. I keep forgetting to meow, and they're talking about ordering out for dinner, since we can't go to the feast."

Sabrina waited. When Valerie didn't say anything more, she said, "And that's a problem?"

"Yes, if what they're going to order is Trash Can Special Number One. I'm under a lot of peer pressure. If we all request the same thing, we get a free order of Kitty Surprise. And believe me, Sabrina, I don't *want* a free order of Kitty Surprise."

"She'd better come with us," Myron said. "She'll never be able to keep up this cheap charade."

"Hey, some confidence in me would be nice," Valerie retorted, obviously insulted.

"Look, there's no time to argue. The third gong has already been rung. We're late, and that's bad," Myron announced. "Bast will notice if you two aren't there. We all have to go."

"But the Love Mirror of Isis is in there. We're so close," Sabrina pleaded.

Myron patted her arm. "Believe me. This is not the time."

Sabrina sighed heavily. Valerie ducked behind a statue and began to pull off her disguise.

"All's not lost yet," Myron added.

"No, not yet," Valerie muttered. "Just in a few more hours."

"Well, as long as we have hope, we have . . . hope," Sabrina pointed out. "So let's keep hoping."

"Yes. Hoping. All the way to the banquet," the *ushabti* said. "Yes?"

"Yes," both girls replied.

"That's the spirit!" Myron cried.

"Whatever," Valerie said dejectedly.

"Ah, there you are," Bast said from her throne as Sabrina, Valerie, and Myron entered the throne room. "We were afraid you'd gotten lost, weren't we, my pet?"

Salem, seated beside the cat goddess, simply stared up at her with total adoration in his big golden eyes. "Am I really your pet?" he gushed. "Oh, I like the sound of that!"

"Humph. Back home, he'd sulk for a week if you called him a pet," Sabrina muttered.

"Yeah, my aunt's calico is the same way," Valerie said.

"Bast has tamed him," Myron said miserably. "Oh, she'll never fall in love with me!"

"Come here and sit at our feet," Bast went on, gesturing with her long gold fingernails. "After all, you will be Salem-hotep's handmaidens for a very, very, very long time to come."

"Gulp," Valerie muttered.

"And me?" Myron asked, as Sabrina carried him toward the throne. "Will I be working for him, too?"

The goddess's eyes narrowed. "That remains to be seen, Myron. As long as he's happy, yes. But if you fail to please him, it's back to the camel stables."

"I'll please him," Myron said eagerly. "Don't worry, your glory. You've picked the right *ushabti* for the job! Have no doubt of that. I'm so happy to—"

"Silence!" Bast shouted. "Must you go on so?"

"Wow, harsh," Sabrina murmured.

Bast glared down at her. "What did you say?"

"Um, harps. I thought I heard harps playing. Didn't you, Valerie?"

"Oh, yes, Harps. And harpsichords."

"What?" Bast frowned at them.

"Not invented yet," Myron mouthed.

"Oh." Sabrina bowed low. "We're just um, excited about the feast, is all. You know, it's not often two kids from the future get a chance to eat dinner with an ancient Egyptian goddess."

"A beautiful ancient Egyptian goddess," Salem added.

"Oh, Salem-hotep," Bast said happily, "you say the most wonderful things."

"I know," he replied, just as happily. "Isn't it wonderful?"

Bast clapped her hands. "Bring Salem-hotep his ankh bread!" she commanded. "We will seal our vows tonight."

"Oh, boy. More of that tasty bread," Salem said, stretching with delight.

"Don't . . ." Sabrina began, then trailed off as everyone looked at her. "Don't forget to, um, save room for dessert," she added nervously.

"Ah. Dessert." The cat goddess raised her chin and smiled at someone across the room.

Sabrina turned to follow her gaze. She was chilled. It was the court magician. He winked at Bast and folded his arms across his chest.

With a flourish of horns and drums, a procession of cat-girls danced into the throne room. One of them carried a large golden platter shaped like a fish. In the center of the platter, lay a sliver of the magical ankh bread.

Sabrina thought long and hard before deciding to trip the cat-girl who carried the platter. She might get turned to stone for her trouble, but at least Salem and Valerie would have a chance to escape.

But just as she extended her foot, the cat-girl danced out of range and knelt in front of Bast. With a *"mrrrow,"* she held out the platter.

The ankh bread twinkled with magic as Bast took it from the platter and held it out to Salem.

"The third token of my undying love for you," Bast told him.

Myron snickered glumly. "Yeah, right," he said under his breath.

Luckily no one heard him but Sabrina. She cleared her throat warningly and he fell silent.

Salem opened his mouth and took the bread from the goddess's hand. He chewed it greedily and swallowed it in one huge gulp.

"Oh, that was so good," he murmured.

Then the goddess clapped her hands, and another procession emerged from the opposite side of the room. Several cat-girls carried jeweled gold boxes, which they opened as they reached the throne.

"Gifts for my beloved," Bast announced.

From the boxes came a collar covered with precious stones, a jewel-encrusted back-scratcher, and a pillow made of the smoothest satin.

"And a gold litter box just for you, my darling," Bast crowed.

"Oh, I'm not worthy!" Salem cried. "How can I ever repay you, my beloved?"

"Just never disappoint me," Bast replied, beaming at him.

"Never fear." Salem's tail switched.

"Ooh, boy," Myron said, sighing. "Here we go again."

"Why are you so sure Salem will ultimately fail?" Valerie asked Myron.

Still gazing at Bast, Myron murmured, "She's the most high-maintenance goddess in the Two Egypts. She's so finicky. Oh, she's *wonderful.*"

Valerie and Sabrina exchanged looks. "Men are so strange," Valerie said. "They should come equipped with a manual."

"Everything else does," Sabrina murmured, thinking of her Witches' Handbook and her magic book. "But half the time that doesn't help much, anyway."

"You have a point." Valerie looked from Bast to Salem to Myron and back to Bast. "But I doubt this kind of thing would be covered."

"Actually, there's a listing for familiar-immortal romances," Sabrina said. "It's on page . . ." She caught herself. She couldn't tell Valerie this! "It's in the book of love." She snapped her fingers. "The book of love, love, love! Isn't that an old song?"

"I wouldn't know it if it was a new one," Valerie said unhappily. "Sabrina, do you realize in the time we've been gone, the face of popular culture may have completely changed?

"I guess there are all kinds of worlds to live in," Sabrina said.

Like this one. Would they be stuck here forever?

☆

Chapter 8

☆

I tried to tell you. I tried to warn you, but oh, do you listen?" the kitchen timer said sternly. "Does anyone ever listen to me?

"Ouch! Well, next time, I will," Hilda groaned, back in their kitchen in Westbridge.

Zelda said, "So will I."

The two sisters were sunburned from head to toe. They had stayed out far too long in the strong sunlight of the French Riviera playing volleyball against Jean-Michel and Vesta. In their shorts and tops, they looked like two Maine lobsters ready and waiting for the butter sauce.

"Let's say it together, then, shall we?" the kitchen timer prodded.

Hilda and Zelda sighed. In unison, they intoned, "Mr. Sun is not our friend."

The timer approved with a vigorous buzz. "Very nice."

"But don't let the sun hear you say that," Zelda murmured, as she put the finishing touches on a sunburn relief potion. She was mixing it in a number 7 cauldron on the counter next to the stove. "All we need is for it to leave the solar system in a huff."

"Ooh, what would happen then?" Hilda asked.

Zelda looked grim. "The immediate cessation of all life as we know it."

"That could be a problem, unless you're a teenager or live with one," Hilda replied, then grinned at her. "Okay, no slamming the sun."

"Speaking of teenagers, it's a good thing Valerie's mother has convinced herself that Valerie's spending the weekend with us," Zelda said.

"Sabrina would never let any harm come to Valerie," Hilda said firmly. "Don't worry, Zel. We'll find them."

"Ah, I feel so refreshed," Vesta announced, swirling into the room in a vivid purple, orange, and red caftan and a matching turban. "It's so nice to shower off all that sand and sunscreen." She fluttered her lashes at her sisters, who in addition to lacking a hunky umbrella holder,

112

had not thought to point some SPF 140 on themselves before the volleyball game.

Vesta peered into the cauldron. "What's that?"

"Burn Away," Hilda said grumpily. "I'll bet we're going to peel."

"Well, look on the bright side," Vesta suggested airily. "Some witches pay a fortune for a chemical peel with that beautician in the Other Realm. You're essentially getting one free!"

"There's that," Zelda said. "Except ours includes ultraviolet skin damage."

"Which we will reverse with our Burn Away," Hilda pointed out. "Mortals are not so lucky."

"No, indeed." Vesta sighed and drummed her nails on the counter. "So has anyone thought of where else we could look for Sabrina? Our twenty-four hours are running out."

"That's for sure," the kitchen timer agreed.

"And you'd be the one to know," Hilda said sweetly, giving the round white timer a little pat. "I just wish you'd stop fretting about everything."

"I admit it. I am a bit of a nag," the timer agreed. "I think it's just that compulsion of mine to keep track of everything, Seconds, minutes, hours . . . it weighs on you after a while." The timer sighed heavily. "I have so many responsibilities."

"Maybe you should delegate," Zelda suggested. "Get someone else to keep track of the seconds, for example."

"We could buy an egg timer to do that," Hilda added. "Would that make life easier for you?"

The timer said, "Give me a minute to consider."

Hilda smiled. "Okay."

"Meanwhile," Zelda announced with a flourish, "our Burn Away is ready. Hildy, you go first."

"Thank goodness."

Hilda picked up the cauldron and drank some of the potion. "Mmm, Zelda, what a nice piña colada taste. Great choice." As she swallowed a little more, her sunburn faded, leaving her a little bit on the pale side, since she'd been indoors so much on council duty.

Hilda handed it to Zelda, who drank some as well. "Not bad, if I do say so." She was even paler, since she'd been indoors reading physics books.

"That almost makes me wish I had a sunburn," Vesta said. "I almost got one while I was in Egypt."

Her eyes widened. "Wait a minute! Sabrina told me she wished we could go to ancient Egypt together just after I packed up my Middle Eastern bazaar and headed for the pleasure dome. Do you suppose that's where she went?" She blinked. "It makes sense!" She tapped her finger against her chin. "I gave her a *ushabti* for a gift."

"Oh, I got one of those for Halloween last year," Hilda said, smiling. "You gave it to me, Zeldy."

Zelda nodded. "That I did. Let's see. Its task was to repack suitcases."

Hilda nodded. "It was a great gift. I can never get everything crammed back in my bags when it's time to go home. Maybe it knows where they went."

"Ding!" the kitchen timer said. "One full minute is up! I say yes to your offer of an egg timer. I'm ready to live a bigger life!"

"Good. Then we'll get one," Hilda told it. "I'm proud of you."

"Thanks." The timer preened.

The three witches trooped upstairs and into Hilda's room. There, stiff-legged on a shelf among some spare crystal balls and a dried corsage from her Quizmaster-student tea, stood her *ushabti*. His face was painted brown and his little Egyptian skirt was a faded but attractive red.

"Hey," Hilda said. "Hi. How've you been?"

The *ushabti* threw her a look. "Pretty bored, to tell you the truth. 'Go to Westbridge, see the world,' they all told me. Almost nine months I've been here, and you haven't gone anywhere."

"That's not true. We just got back from France," Vesta blurted out.

"What?" The *ushabti* was crestfallen.

"But we didn't pack," Hilda assured it. "We stayed just long enough to permanently damage two or three layers of skin."

"That's true," Vesta said. "In their cases."

"Well, all is forgiven, now that we're going somewhere." The figure looked at them skeptically. "We *are* going somewhere, right?"

"Maybe," Hilda said. "If you happen to know where that other *ushabti* went with Sabrina."

"Oh, heck, yes," the *ushabti* said, waving his hand. "The old country. The old, old, very old country. Ask me something I don't know."

The Spellman witches looked at one another wonderingly.

Vesta said, "How *do* you know that?"

"Heard a rumor," he said, shrugging. Then he perked up and eagerly rubbed his hands together. "You know, you should pack a few things for a trip of this magnitude. A few hundred things. Really cram those suitcases full. Come on. I've got some *ushabti* muscles that need flexing."

"What's Sabrina doing in Egypt?" Hilda asked. "Maybe we should just zap her back here."

The *ushabti* shrugged again. "I'm not sure. There's a strike going on at the rumor mill and I didn't get the full report. But I do think she might be in a little bit of trouble. Something to do with the loss of her powers."

"What?" The three sisters looked at him aghast.

"I could be wrong." He held out his hands. "But I could also be right."

"We've got to go to ancient Egypt right away!" Zelda said. "Sabrina needs our help."

"Yes, but how far back should we go?" asked Hilda.

The *ushabti* shrugged. "I didn't say I had all the answers," he pointed out. "Just some of them. What about hiring one of those trolls who finds things?"

"No way. They keep trying to marry Sabrina," Hilda said.

"She is an attractive girl," the *ushabti* said.

"Well, we could start at the beginning of Egyptian history and work our way through it," Zelda suggested. "Maybe we'll figure something out as we go."

Vesta said, "That works for me."

Zelda nodded with determination. "All right. Ladies, start your vacuum cleaners."

"But pack first!" the *ushabti* pleaded.

There were at least three hundred guests at the big feast in Bast's throne room. Only two of them bore no resemblance whatsoever to cats or catlike people. Those two sat as ordered at the feet of Salem-hotep, their weighty cornrow wigs tilted back on their foreheads, their heavy Egyptian eye makeup smudged.

Sabrina's stomach growled as she sat on fat golden pillows and watched a bunch of cat-girls dance. She looked at Valerie and grumbled, "I'm starving."

"That makes sense," Valerie said plaintively, adjusting her wig, "since we've been surrounded by food for four hours and thirty-seven minutes."

If you can call it food, Sabrina thought. The most delectable item on the menu so far had been anchovies and sardines, and Sabrina had never been much of a fan of either.

"What I wouldn't give for some chicken cacciatore," Valerie murmured.

"Well, the dessert should arrive soon," Sabrina said. "And the Love Mirror of Isis along with it. I think one of us should pretend to trip and then break it."

"Can you imagine the bad luck we're going to accumulate?" Valerie asked. "Seven hundred years' bad luck, at least!"

Sabrina gulped. Since she had the most to gain from the breaking of the mirror, she figured she should be the one to do the deed.

"I'll pretend to trip," she offered.

"No, Sabrina, I can't let you do that," Valerie said in a rush. "But since you have a basically sunnier disposition then I do, maybe you could handle all that bad luck better."

"Gee, Val, thanks," Sabrina said sarcastically. She was a little hurt that Valerie had given in so easily.

Valerie grinned at her. "I'm only kidding. Mostly," she said. "I'll tell you what. Let's both pretend to trip at exactly the same time."

"Well, okay," Sabrina agreed, but she was a little skeptical. She might be a witch who was temporarily stripped of her magic powers, but she was still a witch She figured that at some level she had an edge when it came to the effects of magic, even magic created in other times and places. At least having spells and curses cast on her wasn't a total shock, as it was to Valerie. It wouldn't be fair to expose a mortal to the slings and arrows of outrageous spell casting. To quote William Shakespeare, the sixteenth- and seventeenth-century English playwright who had once dated Aunt Zelda.

So she would make sure that she alone broke the mirror when it was brought into the room.

"Hey," she whispered to Myron, who sat on the edge of her pillow and sampled a few tastes of her anchovies, "what's it feel like to be made of stone?"

He thought a moment. Then he gave his chest a sharp tap. "See, the thing is," he began, "I'm not stone, exactly. Clay's a totally different art medium. Stone's very dense. I, on the other hand, am porous."

Sabrina blinked. "Forget I asked."

He held up a hand. "Okay. Let me put it this way." His expression grew soft and wistful, and as he glanced up at Bast, it became positively mournful. "Given a choice between being the most perfect statue at the Museum of Antiquities in Cairo, and some poor creature made of flesh and blood who could send my goddess into gales of laughter . . ." He sighed. "Have you by chance read *Ushabtis Are Made of Clay, Greek Statues Are from Plaster?*"

"Myron," Valerie said, leaning toward him, "I think one of your problems with girls is that you might be just a little on the talkative side."

"Ya think?" he asked.

"I think," both girls said at the same time.

"So. Girls like the strong, silent type," the *ushabti* said, with a tinge of triumph in his voice. "I'll be sure to make a note of that."

His eyes widened. "You're not going to believe this, but the court magician is summoning me," he said. He jerked his head to the left. Sure enough, the magician's large turban bobbed as the tall, white-bearded man gestured at Myron. When the magician's gaze met Sabrina's, he frowned.

Myron said, "Um, I told him I was keeping an

eye on you two. If he finds out I've gone over to the other side . . ."

"We'll make sure he doesn't suspect a thing," Sabrina assured him.

"Good idea, for all our sakes," Myron said.

He slid down from Sabrina's pillow and hurried toward the magician.

Myron tried whistling a happy tune as he approached the court magician.

"Yes, Your Magicalness?" Myron said breathlessly, bowing deeply. "What may I do for you, sir?"

"I found something among the possessions of Salem-hotep's blond handmaiden."

"You went through her things?" Myron asked, a little shocked.

"Do you have a problem with that?" the magician demanded.

"No, no. Of course, you do what you have to do. Um, it's just that I, a mere *ushabti,* would of course not dare to do such a thing, knowing as I do that she is a magical person and fearing that her possessions may be enchanted."

"I took her magic from her and locked it in the mirror," the magician said. "So everything has essentially been decontaminated. Take the object. Examine it."

He bent down and held out a very colorful

bendable rectangle. The images of Sabrina and a young man with extremely large muscles had been printed on the object.

Gingerly Myron held it. He frowned a moment and then realized what it was.

"Oh!" he cried. "It's what they call a photograph—of her and a . . . future boy." He studied the photograph again. "Ah, from my instant dossier, I seem to recall that this is a boy named Harvey. He is her boyfriend."

"Mmm." The magician took back the picture. "Bast is concerned that Salem-hotep might be alarmed if his handmaidens are not happy to remain here in Egypt. Perhaps we should transport this Salem-hotep here."

Myron considered. "But once he looks in the mirror, he won't remember who these handmaidens are. He won't remember anyone from the future."

"But he will see their tears *here*. Perhaps each of them should have a companion."

Myron nodded. "The other one has spoken often of Math Guy. But I don't know who that is."

"Find out by dessert," the magician ordered him.

"Yes, master," Myron said, bowing low.

"And not a word to them of this, or you'll be pebbles by dessert."

Myron gulped. "Yes, sir."

"I'm going to my laboratory. Follow me."

At Mark Clark College in Rhode Island, Harvey Kinkle said, "Hey, you guys. So, like, when you get a shiver down your spine, that means someone's thinking about you, right?"

The guys were in the cafeteria after a long, hard day of football practice. Hamburgers, hot dogs, and chicken breast sandwiches were on the menu, and most Westbridge High football players had eaten two of each.

But Harvey couldn't shake this strange feeling of being connected to someone—as if someone was thinking about him.

It might be Sabrina.

"Dude," said Tom Sniegowski, the Westbridge quarterback, "what it means is that the air conditioning is turned up too high."

Everybody at the big round table laughed, except Harvey, who managed a smile but kept feeling the shiver.

And every time he shivered, he thought about Sabrina.

Then suddenly he was thinking about anchovies and sardines, which was weird, because he would never eat either of those things in a million years.

"Hey, Tommy," one player said to Tom Sniegowski as he walked past their table. "When you called the last play, you said sixty-three instead of fifty-three."

Tom laughed and shook his head. "I always do that. We should just change it. Just call me Math Guy." He shook his head again.

Then Tom shrugged and said to Harvey, "I'm shivering too, Kinkle. It is definitely the air conditioning."

And with that, both guys wolfed down another hamburger and a side of fries.

Down in his laboratory, the court magician nodded to himself.

"I have prepared the concoction that will transport the two companions here. You go back and check on the girls. The companions will materialize near them."

Myron said, "Yes, your twinkliness," and scurried out of the secret room and up the stairway.

He had to tell Sabrina what was going on!

Only five minutes remained until the presentation of the candied catnip dessert. Sabrina whispered to Valerie, "We're too far away. We'll never be able to break the mirror from here."

She sighed. "Although usually that wouldn't be a problem for me."

Valerie looked at her curiously. Sabrina waved her hand. "I mean, because I'm such a klutz."

"You are not. I am," Valerie said loyally. Then she made a little face and said, "Although you could have done better when we tried out for the cheerleading team."

"Woo-hoo! That's it!" Sabrina cried.

She jumped off her pillow and made a big *V* for Victory sign with her arms.

"O great goddess Bast," she said brightly. "My fellow handmaiden and I would like to teach everybody a cheer in honor of you and Salemhotep."

"Sabrina, what are you doing?" Valerie whispered fiercely. "Have you completely lost it?"

"A cheer?" The golden cat goddess narrowed her eyes. "What is a cheer?"

"It's like a . . . a special poem," Sabrina replied. She didn't like the look of those eyes. "Um . . ." She glanced at Valerie. "Help me out, Val."

"Uh. Yeah, a happy, noisy poem," Valerie said. "Which we usually recite at dessert time."

From his pillow beside Bast, Salem cocked his head. "We do not."

"At school we do," Sabrina filled in. "During dessert at school. We just started doing it. It's a brand-new Scallions tradition."

The Westbridge High team was supposed to

have been called the Fighting Stallions, but the printer in charge of the school banner had made an error. The result was that Westbridge became the home of the Fighting Scallions. At least it was different.

"It *is* almost time for dessert," Bast said slowly. "Very well." She relaxed a trifle, leaning against her throne in order to observe.

"Okay!" Sabrina chirped. "Everybody, um, stand up!"

Approximately three hundred cat-people looked at one another, then got to their feet.

"Now watch. Yay!" Valerie shouted, leaping into the air. She nearly landed on her feet, but at the last minute she lost her footing and tumbled onto her behind. Everyone laughed.

"Oh, yes, it's so wonderfully humorous!" Sabrina piped. "Let's all try that on the count of three!"

She and Valerie looked at each other. They bent their knees and clapped their hands.

"One!" they cried together. "Two! Three!"

All the cat people jumped straight up, wobbled, and fell. There were a few meows of pain, but most of the crowd looked ready to try it again.

"Let's do that again. Yay!" Valerie shouted. This time, however, she landed perfectly on her feet. Surprised, she looked at Sabrina and said, "Whoops."

"How is this a poem?" Bast demanded. Her eyes began to glow again.

"Oh, the poem. We were just warming up," Sabrina told her. "Let's see. The poem goes like this. Everybody watch first, then imitate me."

She tried to remember some of the routines she had seen Libby Chessler and her cheerleading squad do. First she flung her arms out to the sides and cried, *"S!* Which looks like a *T,* but is an *S!"*

Then she made an upside-down *V* and cried, "A! Which stands for 'absolutely adorable'!"

Valerie took Sabrina's lead. *"L,* which means 'lovely'!"

Sabrina stood sideways and extended one arm at an angle, then extended the other one straight out, added a leg, and cried, *"E,* because he exercises!"

"And he's excellent!" Valerie added quickly.

Sabrina picked up the cheer again. "And *M,* which I have no idea how to make, which stands for 'magnificent'!"

"Put them all together, they spell"—Valerie paused abruptly—"Sabrina, they spell . . . 'Mirror'!"

"What?" Sabrina cried, then looked to her left and right, and then behind her.

The Love Mirror of Isis was in Bast's lap!

While they had been cheering, the court magician must have magically transported the mirror into the goddess's hands. And now she was holding it up, petting Salem, and turning his head toward the mirror.

Sabrina shouted, "Put it all together, it spells 'Salem, don't look!'"

She dived for the mirror just as Salem looked into it. Bast leaped off the throne and thundered, "How dare you!"

At the same time, Salem blinked up at Bast and said, "Who am I? I don't care. I love you!"

And two seconds later, in a puff of blue smoke, Tom Sniegowski, the Scallions' starting quarterback, appeared in the center of the throne room.

"Whoa, where am I?" he shouted, whirling in a circle.

One second later, in another puff of blue smoke and a flash of lightning, Harvey appeared.

"Harvey!" Sabrina cried. "What are you doing here?"

And one more second later, in one more puff of blue smoke, a flash of lightning, and a clap of thunder, a third visitor materialized.

Sabrina stared.

It was Willard Kraft, the vice-principal of Westbridge High!

"Okay, detention for everyone," he said uncertainly. "Whoever spiked my apple juice is in *huge* trouble."

"Who are these people?" Bast shouted.

"Who cares? I love you," Salem repeated.

The court magician came forward. "I wished to provide the handmaidens with companions," he explained. "So that they would not pine."

"Pine," the goddess said angrily. "I'll turn them all into trees!" She pointed at Sabrina and Valerie. "You were trying to steal the mirror, weren't you?"

"Yes, but for Salem's sake," Valerie cried, raising her chin, at the exact same time Sabrina said, "No way."

Valerie made a face. "Oops."

Bast was furious. "You will pay! I will turn you to stone!"

Harvey moved closer to Sabrina and murmured, "Um, I have the feeling we're not in Rhode Island anymore." He looked around. "But then, it's hard to tell. That university has a nice campus. This does look like the cafeteria, kind of."

Tom Sniegwoski murmured, "Mommy."

Just then Myron hurried up to the base of the throne. He bowed low several times, holding out his arms.

"Your vast Bastness," he said, "please. Turning them to stone is better than they deserve. Trust me. Being turned to stone is not that bad."

Bast glared down at him with her brilliant golden eyes.

"It's a pretty good life," he went on. "Here's a thought. Why not send them all back to the future? It's horrible there. They have all kinds of modern conveniences and they get to—I mean, they have to—do horrible things, like watch television."

"Really," she said, her eyes beginning to lose their glow.

He nodded vigorously. "And since I did such a terrible job of guarding the handmaidens, maybe you should send me there with them!"

"Oh, I'll send all of you somewhere," she said, with an evil laugh. "Court magician!"

"Front and center," the court magician said anxiously. "Yes, Oh Pawful One."

"Transport them all to the Great Pyramid! Immediately!"

"Salem, stop them!" Sabrina cried.

Salem opened his mouth. He blinked. Then he looked up at Bast and said, "I adore you."

Poof!

Suddenly Sabrina found herself in a small, dark place with at least four other people.

She thought maybe it was a cave.

"Sabrina?" Harvey said in the blackness. "Where are we?"

"Um, a cave?" she answered.

"Oy, are we in trouble." It was Myron. Sabrina felt him tapping on her sandal.

"Why, Myron?" she asked, bending down and scooping him up.

"Because this is the Great Pyramid, future

burial site of the current pharaoh . . . and there's no way out!"

"Sabrina Spellman, I don't know what kind of trick this is. I have no idea how you managed all this. But you are in such big trouble," Mr. Kraft said. "If I ever find you, I'm going to give you detention for a thousand years."

"Don't worry, buddy," Myron said unhappily. "She'll be here a lot longer than that."

Myron sighed. "And so will the rest of us."

"Not good news," Sabrina murmured.

Not good news at all.

Chapter 9

Sabrina shuffled forward slowly, hands out in front of her, and muttered, "This is the pits."

"No," Myron said on her shoulder. "These are the Many Small Rooms of Doom. The pits are down the hall on your right. Excuse me." Sabrina felt him scramble off her shoulder and thud onto the dirt floor.

"Sabrina, what kind of perfume are you wearing?" Harvey asked from the musty darkness. "You smell great."

"Mr. Kinkle, please! I am your vice-principal! And I am an Aqua Velva man!"

"Excuse me, sir, but that's not me," Harvey said.

"Cool your jets, Jack," Myron huffed. "I got

confused in the dark. I thought you were Sabrina."

Someone slipped his hand into Sabrina's.

"Sabrina?" Harvey murmured into her ear.

"Harvey." She would have smiled at him if he could have seen her. And if she had been happy. "I'm glad you're here, but I'm sorry, too," she said.

"Yeah. It's kind of like being on a bad date," he said, then added quickly, "not that we've ever been on a bad date."

"It's like having a fight," she said, then added, "but we've never really had a fight, either."

She tried again. "What I mean, Harvey, is that I'm sorry you're stuck in this tiny room of doom with me." She paused. "I'm guessing that you probably don't realize you've been magically transported to ancient Egypt."

"Wow. No. I didn't realize that."

"What?" Mr. Kraft cried. "This isn't some crazy high school prank?"

"Mr. Kraft," Sabrina said, "toilet-papering your house is a crazy high school prank. Whisking you off to ancient Egypt is a little more serious."

"I can't believe this," Mr. Kraft whispered to himself. "I've gone completely insane!"

"That's what *I* thought," Valerie said. "No. Actually, I thought I was dreaming."

"Tom?" Harvey said.

"Ooph. I think he fainted," Valerie announced. "Or I just stumbled over someone else who is lying unconscious on the floor."

"Hey, pssst, Myron," came another voice.

"Benny? My man! Is that you?" Myron asked excitedly. "Benny from Delphi?"

"The same."

"Snap it, big guy," Myron said.

There was a clicking noise, and suddenly the room was brilliant with light. It was a very small room, and all the walls were decorated with brilliant paintings of people in profile being mangled or stabbed by arrows, axes, or spears.

"Okay, what just happened?" Mr. Kraft asked. He was dressed for tennis, in white shorts and a white V-necked sweater over a white shirt. Beside Sabrina, Harvey was in his football uniform. On the ground, Tom Sniegowski—who was indeed unconscious—was also wearing his uniform.

Myron bounded over to the other *ushabti* and threw his arms around him. "Benny! What are you doing here?"

Benny stuck out his chest very importantly. "Well, it's all very hush-hush, but I'm sure I can tell you." He paused for dramatic effect. "We're here with the big guy."

"No! Get out!" Myron said excitedly.

"It's true. It's true." Benny pretended to yawn, then grinned at Myron. "Isn't that nifty?"

"Excuse me, excuse me," Mr. Kraft said, elbowing his way past Harvey and over to the two *ushabti*. "I'm an authority figure, and I demand to know exactly what's going on."

Myron patted Benny. "Well, you see, master," he began. Mr. Kraft smiled at the use of the word "master," obviously pleased. "We're part of a vast *ushabti* network."

"Without us, Egypt would fall apart," Benny added grandly. "We keep the whole joint running."

Myron continued, "Benny's task is to light up dark places."

"And we're all over this Pyramid," Benny said excitedly. "With *him*."

"*Him* whom?" Mr. Kraft asked sternly.

"*Him* the pharaoh," Benny said. He thrust out his chest. "He came to check out his tomb. You see," he said to Mr. Kraft, "here in Egypt, after you die, you get a big, fancy resting place like this. *If* you're one of the rich and famous."

Myron nodded. "Which the pharaoh is."

"Most assuredly which the pharaoh is." He sniffed. "Who's wearing Simply Irresistible?"

"Yeah, what is that stuff?" Harvey asked. "It's great."

Valerie and Sabrina smiled at each other and giggled.

"Well, I demand that you take us to the pharaoh," Mr. Kraft said. "He'll certainly know the way out of his own tomb!"

Benny made a face and turned to Myron. "I have good news and bad news."

Myron frowned. "Go ahead, Benny. Lay it on me."

Benny said, "The pharaoh's lost, too. We've been looking for a way out for two days."

Everybody groaned.

"And the good news?" Sabrina asked hopefully.

"Well, the pharaoh said he's supposed to end up here eventually, so if he dies in here, he'll have saved himself a trip."

Everybody groaned again.

The group in the Room of Doom cheered up a little at the next thing Benny the *ushabti* said: "It's really not too likely that any of you are going to die in this joint. The pharaoh brought at least a hundred of us with him. Some of us are in charge of water, some in charge of food, and then there are the specialists, like me. Oh, and puzzle solvers. Really good ones."

He winked at Sabrina. "Not for nothing is my boss Lord of the Two Lands. He comes equipped for any emergency. Why, he even has *ushabti* who specialize in dates and honeys."

Sabrina was confused. "You mean, like different types of dates?

Benny laughed. "No, I mean honeys to date. Like you and the other little honey over there." He pointed at Valerie.

"Hey, wait a minute," Harvey said. "Sabrina and I are going steady."

Benny shrugged, looking totally unimpressed as he gave Harvey the once-over. "And what are you, some kind of strangely built person? Bachelor Number Two is a mighty king."

"He has on his football gear," Sabrina said loyally. "That's why he looks strange."

Benny cocked his head. "Bad hair, too. My master's got a nice head of black curls. Everybody keeps telling him to shave it off—that's the fashion these days. But not my big guy."

"Sounds cute," Valerie said. "I'd like to meet him."

Benny bowed low. "In that case, follow me."

Everybody looked at each other, then at the *ushabti.*

"I have no doubt this room is booby-trapped," Mr. Kraft said. "It being in an Egyptian tomb and all."

"Oh, pshaw." Benny snickered. "Here's the big booby trap: You have to crawl out through that door on your hands and knees." He pointed to a small square cut into the wall. "If you *walk* over the pressure plate in front of that door, a hundred thousand darts will shoot from the walls and inject poison into you. You'll die horribly but quickly."

Sabrina looked at Harvey, who looked back at her with huge eyes. He gave her hand a squeeze and said, "This is a lot worse than football practice."

"Well, I suggest we get going," Mr. Kraft said. He got down on his hands and knees. "We haven't got all day."

"It's night, Mr. Kraft," Harvey said.

"Okay," Mr. Kraft said, sighing with impatience. "We haven't got all night."

"Actually, Valerie and I have," Sabrina said unhappily. "Since Salem looked into the Love Mirror of Isis, we're stuck here in ancient Egypt forever."

"Actually, we have one more chance to reverse that," Myron said, holding up a hand. "Tonight is the Night of the Scarab Moon. After tonight, the spell will become irreversible. But if we can get that mirror and focus the moon's rays in it, all the spells captured in the mirror will be broken."

"Woo-hoo!" Sabrina cried.

"And your master has been stuck in here for how long?" Mr. Kraft asked Benny. "Two days? And we have how long?"

"Oh, about two hours," Myron said, sounding glum. "You have a point, man of the future."

Sabrina rubbed her hands together. "Well, all we can do is try, right, Valerie?" Valerie nodded. "Harvey, are you with us?"

"That's a big high five, Sabrina," Harvey said.

They high-fived each other.

"Mom, is it time to get up?" Tom Sniegowski said, lifting his head from the floor.

With Benny in the lead and Myron bringing up the rear, Sabrina and the others navigated the twists and turns of the pyramid. Other *ushabti* joined them, offering them food and drink and methods of avoiding the traps in the various rooms.

For example, Abe the *ushabti* explained that in the next Room of Doom, they had to avoid the diamond-shaped stones on the floor and step only on the square ones, or the entire ceiling would collapse on them. In the room after that, each person had to answer, "What is the best color in the universe?" by pressing on a big green eye painted in a corner of the room. (Green was the pharaoh's favorite color.)

Rachel, a female *ushabti,* told them that in the Corridor of Dreams, they had to hold their breath and tiptoe past a statue of a sleeping old man. If it detected any vibrations or noise, the statue would "awaken" and a huge rolling ball would rumble down the corridor and crush them all.

Next came a sand pit, which they could avoid only by leaping across it.

After successfully making it through several more puzzles and traps, they were greeted by at least a dozen very dour-looking *ushabti* with painted-on Egyptian guard uniforms, who asked Benny for the password—which was harum-scarum—and then demanded to know who all of the others were and what they were doing here.

"And who's wearing Simply Irresistible?" one of them asked Benny.

"The honeys," Benny replied.

The guard nodded and said, "Good."

Benny turned to the others and held up both his hands.

"This is big stuff, folks," he said. "We are now entering the burial chamber where my main master, the pharaoh himself, will be laid to rest when he dies. Unfortunately, he's stuck in there now, and he's very much alive. He cannot decipher the puzzle, and neither can any of the *ushabti*. He has declared that he will offer a boon to anyone who solves the riddle and gets us all out of here."

"What's a boon?" Harvey asked.

"This is such a weird dream," Tom Sniegowski muttered to himself, rubbing the back of his head.

"A favor," Mr. Kraft said. He smiled. "And as the best-educated individual here, I'm sure to receive it."

"Let's hope so, bubie," Myron told him. "Because if you guess wrong, the chamber will burst into flame and all of us will be burned to a crisp."

"Or maybe I'll just keep my mouth shut," Mr. Kraft muttered.

"Whatever." Benny clapped his hands. "Remember, everybody: in ancient Egypt, the pharaoh is the closest thing to a rock star. Let's act accordingly."

Valerie tapped Sabrina on the shoulder. "Does he mean we should ask the pharaoh for autographs?"

"No, just suck up to him a lot," Sabrina said.

The girls nodded in unison.

"We're going in," Benny announced.

The *ushabti* guards parted into two rows, and Benny led Sabrina and the others into the pharaoh's dangerous burial chamber.

Zelda got off her vacuum cleaner, stood on the edge of time, and folded her arms across her chest. The sands of time lay before them, vast plains and curved dunes beneath an eternal field of twinkling stars.

"Girls," she said, "I don't think Sabrina's in the Old Kingdom period after all." She tapped her foot on the power control. "I suggest we move to the Eleventh Dynasty."

"Middle Kingdom?" Vesta queried, considering. "And skip the First Intermediate Period altogether?"

Hilda grimaced and whispered to the *ushabti*, "Boy, I wish I'd paid closer attention in history class."

The *ushabti*, whose name was Nate, waved his hand in dismissal. "Don't sweat it. I lived through all these kingdoms and periods and I still can't keep them straight."

Hilda brightened a little. "On the other hand, I can name all the U.S. Presidents in order."

"There you go," the *ushabti* said cheerily. "If you ever get lost in American history, you'll be all set!"

"Yeah." She smiled broadly. "I can hardly wait!"

Just then, another *ushabti* appeared on the horizon astride a tiny clay horse. The horse was very cracked and had been glued back together at least once or seventeen times.

The rider gave Nate a wave and dismounted.

"You the future people looking for some other future people being held prisoner in the past?"

Zelda eagerly nodded. "Yes, yes, we are!"

"Well, I have news for you. They're in a more

futuristic past than here. You want to go to the Sweet Sixteenth Dynasty. So named because the pharaoh ascended the throne when he was sixteen. He's currently eighteen."

"Oh, good!" Zelda smiled at him. "This is so kind of you."

"Don't mention it." He winked at her. "I got family working for that pharaoh. Three hundred and twenty-seven cousins, in fact. Well, I have to get back to work. I'm in charge of the toy stable of this bratty royal princess. She doesn't know the difference between breaking in a horse and breaking it into small pieces. Right, Ra?"

The horse nickered.

"Oh, I'm so sorry," Zelda said.

"It's okay. Ra's a tough old clay horse. Hey, Nate, be cool."

The helpful *ushabti* climbed back onto the horse and cantered away.

"Okay. Sweet Sixteenth Dynasty, here we come!" Vesta cried.

☆

Chapter 10

☆

Sabrina's group filed into the pharaoh's burial chamber and found a young man seated on the edge of a large carved sarcophagus shaped like a mummy. Long, curly hair tumbled over his shoulders. His face was very tan, his cheekbones high, and his dark eyes flashed with interest as he looked at the two girls. When he smiled, his teeth flashed a brilliant white.

"Wow, Sabrina," Valerie whispered, "he's so *cute.*"

"Exactly," Benny said, extending his arms and bowing very low to the man. "Mere commoners, allow me to introduce you to my master, the great pharaoh Kutanthansum!"

Sabrina couldn't help her grin. The pharaoh's

name sounded exactly like "cute and hand-some." Which he was.

Beside her, Harvey kind of growled. She grinned even more broadly. Harvey was jealous of him!

"Mmm, who's wearing Simply Irresistible?" the pharaoh said by way of greeting. "Because it is. I shall take the wearer of that sweet perfume for a spin in my dune chariot!"

"Me!" Valerie cried, raising her hand. Then she looked guiltily at Sabrina and said, "And so is she!"

"Um, master, excuse me," Benny ventured, "but nobody's going for a spin anywhere until we solve the riddle of your burial chamber."

"Oh, that's right." He frowned at the girls. "Sorry."

"Well, maybe we can solve it together," Sabrina suggested, smiling at him. "What is it?"

Poof!

Just then, Sabrina's aunts, Vesta, Hilda, and Zelda magically appeared in the chamber.

"Sabrina darling!" Vesta cried, running to embrace Sabrina. "We've been so worried about you!"

"Aunts!" Sabrina hugged all three in turn. "How did you ever find us?"

"With a little help from some little friends," Hilda said, holding up a *ushabti*. "Especially this guy."

"But you're for repacking," Benny said to the newcomer. "They don't have any luggage."

"Tell me about it," he pouted. "They tricked me."

Vesta tapped the figurine on the nose. "Darling, don't you worry. I will not leave this dynasty without at least a dozen suitcases brimming with wonderful things to clutter up the pleasure dome. And I'll personally unpack them all before we go home, so that you'll have plenty to do while we sit by the pool." She glanced around. "Or whatever passes for a pool around here."

"Lotus pond," Sabrina said.

Vesta clapped her hands. "How wonderfully exotic!"

"Now, Vesta, remember, no tanning," Zelda said.

Vesta cleared her throat. "If you'd just remember to put on some sunscreen first, you'd be fine."

Hilda joined in. "There's no such thing as safe tanning."

"Ladies, ladies," Myron said nervously. "Excuse me, but you're in the presence of exalted greatness. This is the great pharaoh Kutanthansum."

"I'll say," Vesta drawled, fluttering her eyelashes.

"See, we're stuck in here until we solve the

great riddle," Sabrina said, and proceeded to explain everything.

"So what's the riddle?" Zelda asked. "We're smart. We can solve it."

Everyone looked at Kutanthansum. He pointed above his head. One half of the ceiling was painted like the night sky, with a brilliant moon and silver and blue stars. The other side of the ceiling was painted with a brilliant sun and a few wispy clouds.

"The riddle is 'Which is my friend'?"

"Well, certainly not Mr. Sun," Sabrina said without thinking. Her eyes widened as she looked at her three aunts. "Aunt Hilda! Aunt Zelda! Aunt Vesta! That's got to be it!"

The young pharaoh scratched his head. "How can that be it? That doesn't make any sense to me."

Mr. Kraft stepped forward. "Well, you see, young man, in the future, we know about ultraviolet light and . . ." He trailed off. His eyes bulged as he made little steps in a circle and stared at the friezes on the walls. "It just occurred to me. We really are in ancient Egypt!"

"No, it's all just a dream," Tom said, nodding at Harvey. "Right, Kinkle?"

"Um, sure, Tom." He looked at Sabrina.

"Sure," she said brightly. How on earth was she ever going to explain all this if they ever got back to Westbridge?

"Well, if you all think that's the correct answer," Pharaoh Kutanthansum said, "let's give it a try. The worst thing that can happen is that we'll all be burned to a cinder." He smiled dreamily at Sabrina and Valerie. "At least I'll die smelling that divine fragrance."

"Charred human flesh?" Hilda asked, making a face.

"Simply Irresistible," he murmured.

Then he stood up and touched the large painted face of the sun.

Immediately music began to play and the ceiling opened up, revealing the Egyptian night sky.

"Oh, gosh, look at the moon!" Sabrina cried.

There on the face of the full moon was the outline of a large beetle.

"That's the Scarab Moon," Pharaoh Kutanthansum said. "And on the Night of the Scarab Moon lovers' wishes come true forever."

Harvey looked at Sabrina. "Then I wish—"

"Careful," Sabrina said anxiously.

"I wish for whatever you wish for," he said, looking nervous.

She closed her eyes. "Okay, I wish for a plan to save Salem and take care of, um, my situation, and that we all go back to Westbridge and I'm not in trouble with anybody."

"How could you be in trouble, Sabrina?"

Valerie asked. "You didn't make any of this happen."

"That's technically true," she said to her aunts.

The young pharaoh held out his arms.

"Then if we are to do all these things, we must leave my pyramid at once," he said. "Onward to adventure!"

After they escaped from the Great Pyramid of Kutanthansum, it was a much less complicated matter to jump into a few of the pharaoh's chariots and gallop across the desert sands to Bast's palace. On the way, Sabrina and Valerie, who rode with the pharaoh, concocted a scheme to save Salem. Sabrina hoped it would save her powers, too, but she kept that part to herself.

"I love it!" the pharaoh announced, holding the reins of his two ebony horses as Valerie and Sabrina hung on to him, one on either side. "It's so zany! I never get to do anything zany anymore." He winked at her. "Believe me, being a pharaoh is a lot less fun than it looks."

"So you'll do it?" Sabrina said.

He threw back his head and laughed. "Heck, yeah!"

Valerie leaned around him and said to Sabrina, "Don't you find it rather odd that we're all speaking modern English?"

Sabrina shrugged. "They don't worry about that on *Star Trek*. Why should we?"

"Good point." Valerie smiled at Sabrina and mouthed, *He's cuter than Math Guy.*

Then they were there. While the *ushabti* dealt with the chariots and the horses, Vesta pointed up a large trunk filled with beautiful costumes and musical instruments. They all set about disguising themselves.

As Harvey pulled on a turban, he asked, "So what did you and Valerie talk about with that pharaoh guy?"

"We've thought of a way to save Salem," Sabrina informed him.

Harvey cocked his head. "Save him from what? He looked to me as if he was having a pretty good time."

"Yeah, well, you tend to look that way if you're hypnotized or enchanted," Sabrina said with authority. Then she caught herself and said, "Um, so I've heard."

"Well, I'm enchanted," Harvey said, grinning at her. "Do I look as if I'm having a good time?"

"Considering the fact that you've been magically whisked to ancient Egypt, I'd have to go with a yes," Sabrina replied, grinning back.

"Well, I'm going with the 'this is all a dream' scenario," he explained, looking earnest. "Valerie's wavering, but your aunts and Mr. Kraft have pretty much decided it's either that or we're going to get rich after we appear on *Sightings.*"

He rubbed his hands together. "So what's the plan to break Salem out of honeymoon prison?"

Sabrina dug into the trunk. "We're a troupe of entertainers," she said. She handed him a long robe to wear. "How's your tambourine-playing?"

"Better than my pass-receiving," he replied, holding the robe up to himself. "This looks like a dress."

"You'll look great in it," she assured him. "It goes great with the turban."

"If you say so." Harvey was very easygoing. That was one of the things Sabrina liked about him

"Aunt Vesta, would you dress up like Scheherazade?" Sabrina asked her aunt. She twirled in a circle holding out a very glittery halter top and a pair of silk harem pants.

"Oh, absolutely! What divine clothes," Vesta crooned, sweeping over to her niece.

She smiled at Mr. Kraft. "And you would look terrific dressed as the fire eater." She showed him an abbreviated one-piece leopard-skin tunic and a pair of sandals that curled up at the toes.

"You think so?" He stuck out his chest and came to collect his outfit.

"Oh, absolutely," Vesta assured him. "All the girls will go wild."

Soon they were dressed up like traveling entertainers. The pharaoh, in a caftan and a false beard, was their leader, and it was he who requested entrance to Bast's throne room. They stood just outside the gates, in the glow of the Scarab Moon, as the grand vizier came to look them over. To Sabrina's relief, he didn't appear to recognize Valerie or her.

"We have heard that Bast has married a wonderful cat," Kutanthansum said in a thick accent that sounded vaguely French. "And we would love to help her celebrate."

The grand vizier shrugged and said. "Sure. Why not? It'll be fun. Hold on. Let me see."

He came back moments later and said, "The great goddess Bast has agreed. Come in!"

Sabrina looked at Valerie and the two friends crossed their fingers.

"Well, here goes nothing," Sabrina said excitedly.

Woo-hoo!

Chapter 11

As Pharaoh Kutanthansum led the "troupe" into Bast's throne room, the grand vizier announced, "O Great Goddess, allow me to present these miserable performers, who wish to celebrate your auspicious wedding day by boring you with their third-rate dances and songs." He clapped his hands three times. "Presenting the Troupe of the Desert!"

Bast and Salem were lounging on the throne, Salem in Bast's lap. As the other cat-people seated at long wooden tables politely applauded, the servants continued to bring them huge platters of food and bowls of drink.

Salem kept looking up at Bast with a dazed,

happy expression, while Bast gestured for Sabrina and the others to come forward.

"How kind," she said. "I hope you're worth the interruption. Unlike our previous entertainers, who have been dealt with. Permanently."

Sabrina swallowed.

Everyone in the throne room sat back to watch the show. The "entertainers" glanced at each other uncertainly. *Whoops.* They hadn't actually gotten as far as planning what to do!

Then Zelda stepped forward and started singing a song: "Some enchanted evening you may meet a stranger." She gestured for the others to join in.

Sabrina blinked. She had never heard this song in her life. But Mr. Kraft, Hilda, and Vesta knew it. They took up the melody. After a few bars, Harvey started beating his tambourine. The pharaoh had slung a long cylindrical drum on a strap over his shoulder and was pounding out the rhythm. Tom picked up a flute and blew on it every once in a while.

Sabrina shrugged. "I guess we're dancers," she said to Valerie.

"Which is very much like being cheerleaders again," Valerie replied.

They began to whirl around in circles, stumbling a little as they watched each other.

"Hey, you're making me dizzy!" Myron said in a stage whisper. "I think I might throw up!"

"Not in my pocket, *please*," Sabrina begged. Then she stumbled and collided with Valerie.

Sabrina whirled out of control, spinning like a top in the opposite direction. Then suddenly she saw the court magician. He was carrying something beneath a heavy black blanket. It was the exact size and shape of the Love Mirror of Isis!

Sabrina whirled and twirled her way toward the throne. As the rest of the troupe watched, puzzled, she spun toward the magician and grabbed the edge of the covering. As everyone gasped, the cover tumbled to the floor.

The court magician, however, kept hold of the mirror, and Bast jumped to her feet and cried, "No! Salem-hotep, don't look!"

But Sabrina did look.

In the mirror, the Scarab Moon glowed brightly. The Scarab was clearly outlined in black on the brilliant disk.

As Sabrina stared, she felt herself tingle. She held out her hands and saw that they were sparkling with magic.

"Woo-hoo!" she cried.

"The spell is reversed!" Bast cried. She shook her finger at the court magician. "I *told* you to take that thing away before the moon rose tonight!"

So looking into the Love Mirror of Isis a second time on the Night of the Scarab Moon reversed the spells it cast?

On a hunch, Sabrina pointed Salem off the throne and levitated him so that he had to look directly into the mirror.

A hush went over the throne room as Salem stared at the magical reflection of the Scarab Moon. Then he shook himself and said, "Huh? Sabrina? What's going on?"

He looked at Bast. "How are you, beautiful?" he asked.

Bast threw back her head. "No!" she cried.

She pointed at the magician. "For this blunder, I will turn you and all men in here to stone!"

Then Myron popped his head out of Sabrina's pocket and said, "Now, wait just a darn minute! That's enough, Bast!"

Bast shook with rage. "How dare you?" she bellowed at Myron.

"I dare because I care about you," he said. "You're the unhappiest goddess I've ever seen, because you're looking for love in all the wrong places."

"Hey," Salem said, insulted.

"I've loved you for centuries," Myron said firmly. "If you were my wife, I would treat you like, well, a goddess, yes, but also like a queen."

"You . . . insolent—" Bast sputtered.

Then Sabrina pointed at Myron. Instantly, he was transformed into a very feline man. His hair was a tawny mane, and his skin was golden. His almond-shaped eyes were a brilliant green.

He stomped up the steps to the throne and put his hands on his hips. "You were saying . . . ?" he demanded of Bast.

Bast's mouth worked, but no sound came out. She was obviously completely bowled over by Myron.

"Oh, Myron," she said finally.

"I am Myron no longer." His voice was deep and throaty. "I am Amun-Lobo."

"Oh, wow," Bast said.

"Yeah," Hilda, Valerie, Zelda, and Vesta chorused.

"Hey," said Harvey, the pharaoh, Tom, and Mr. Kraft.

"And I love you," Bast said.

Amun-Lobo said, "That may be, Bast, but you have acted like a spoiled child for millennia. I demand that you release all the men and cats you have turned into stone, and that you promise here and now never to use that spell again."

She fluttered her lashes at him. "Oh, Amun-Lobo, I do promise. I do!"

"Very well. Then I shall kiss you," he announced.

And he did.

Bast swooned.

Everyone in the palace sighed and went "Awwwww."

As soon as Bast could speak again, she approached Sabrina.

"Can you ever forgive me for stealing your magic and sealing you and your friends up in a tomb, to die there of thirst and hunger?"

"Ah, that'd be a maybe," Sabrina allowed, grimacing. Her secret had been revealed in front of mortals. How was she ever going to explain to the Witches' Council?

If she ever even saw the council again.

"Stealing your magic, Sabrina?" Mr. Kraft cried. "You're witches? I knew it! I knew there was something about you Spellmans!"

"Sabrina, why didn't you ever tell Harvey and me?" Valerie demanded.

Sabrina bit her lower lip. "Actually, I have, a couple of times, but I magically made you forget." She looked at Bast. "You see, Your Goddessness, we witches are supposed to keep our magical powers suppressed when we're among, ah, non-witch types."

"Oh, dear. What must I do to atone for my actions?" Bast asked Sabrina, covering her mouth.

Amun-Lobo took Bast's hand and raised it to his lips. "That would be simple, my love. Return them to their own time, and erase from the minds of the mortals all knowledge of the fact that this girl and her aunts are witches."

"Oh, you're so very clever," Bast said to Amun-Lobo.

"And I want to go with them," the pharaoh

said, removing his disguise. "I'm bored and I want an adventure."

"Oh, Kutanthansum," Bast said, inclining her head, "Lord of the Two Lands!" She smiled at them all. "Your wish is my command."

It was a Saturday night in Westbridge, about a month later. It was midnight at the Oasis, the new, very fancy mansion on the edge of town, owned by a handsome young newcomer named Kurt Hanson. Nearly all of the Westbridge High students were there, dancing to an excellent band called the Pharaohs.

"Wow, Sabrina, where did you and Valerie meet this guy?" Libby Chessler asked, as she admired the Egyptian art with which the wealthy young man had decorated his enormous home.

"Oh, we just ran into him," Sabrina said.

"Well, he's . . . he's so cute and handsome," Libby murmured, wandering off in a daze. "But I can't figure out why he's so nice to a freak and a geek."

"Yeah." Valerie blinked. "How come he's so nice to us?" She blinked again. "I can't really remember how we *did* meet him, Sabrina."

"At the pet shop, remember?"

"Oh. Right." Valerie frowned, concentrating. "Something about a cat. Salem got stuck in the pet store."

"Right."

Just then, Hilda and Zelda sauntered by. Zelda smiled at the girls, and Hilda gave Sabrina a little wink.

Then Valerie brightened as Tom Sniegowski approached. "Look. This guy is so cute. Much cuter than the other guy I had an unrequited crush on."

Sabrina pointed at Valerie again. Tom sniffed the air.

"Mmm, you smell so good," he said to Valerie. "Wanna dance?"

Valerie's eyes got huge. "Sure!"

The two bopped away.

Salem stood behind a palm tree, whapping a tambourine with his tail. As Sabrina came up to him, he gestured toward the crowded dance floor.

Bast and Amun-Lobo were slow-dancing to a very fast song. They saw Sabrina and Salem and waved. Bast moved her left hand, and a huge diamond wedding ring sparkled in the light. Sabrina waved back happily.

"I guess Bast and her new cat's-paw dropped by for a few dances," Salem said pensively. "She'll always be the one, Sabrina."

Uh-oh. Hadn't the spell been reversed?

"The one that I got away from," Salem finished with an ironic drawl.

Sabrina laughed. Salem joined her, then

quieted as Harvey half-walked, half-danced toward them.

"Some summer, eh, Sabrina?" he said, as he handed her a root beer.

"Sure was," Sabrina replied, clinking soda cans with him. "And you know what? Amazingly enough, I can't wait for school to start!"

About the Author

Best-selling author NANCY HOLDER has sold thirty-six novels, including *Sabrina the Teenage Witch: Spying Eyes* and, with her frequent co-author, Christopher Golden, *Buffy the Vampire Slayer: The Watcher's Guide*. She has also sold over two hundred short stories, articles, and essays. Her work has been translated into more than two dozen languages, and she has received four Bram Stoker awards for her supernatural fiction.

A native Californian, she lives in San Diego with her husband, Wayne, and their daughter, Belle. In her spare time she works out at the gym. A confirmed bookaholic, she can't pass a bookstore without going in, and she can't go in without buying something. Luckily, she considers reading, as well as watching TV, a part of her job as a freelance writer. It's also one of the few professions that pay her to daydream.

Her next Sabrina novel, *Up, Up, and Away,* will be available soon.

American S·I·S·T·E·R·S

Join different sets of sisters
as they embark on the varied,
sometimes dangerous,
always exciting journeys
that crossed America's landscape!

West Along the Wagon Road, 1852

❧

A Titanic Journey Across the Sea, 1912

❧

Voyage to a Free Land, 1630

❧

Adventure on the Wilderness Road, 1775

By Laurie Lawlor

A MINSTREL® BOOK
Published by Pocket Books   2106

2070